PURSUIT

By
J. Wayne Frye

Published in Canada

PURSUIT

THE AUTHOR

Wayne Frye's *Aaron Adams, Girl* series books and *Lynton* adventures are popular among mystery readers. He writes satirical political commentary for newspapers and his books on politics have created a great deal of controversy. He has written marketing/advertising textbooks, been a highly successful U.S. university hockey coach, professor, university president and served as a marketing consultant to hockey teams and motion picture companies. He has been cited for his work with inner-city gang children in the Los Angeles area and been active in the anti-globalization movement. He became a Canadian citizen in 2003 and lives in Ladysmith, British Columbia and Cavite, Philippines.

Other Books by J. Wayne Frye

Hockey Mania and the Mystery of Nancy Running Elk
Something Evil in the Darkness at Hopkins House
How Hockey Saved a Jew From the Holocaust:
The Rudi Ball Story
The Catastrophic Calamities of a Village Idiot
Fighting for Justice in the Land of Hypocrisy
Guide to Alternative Education (13 Editions)
White Meteors and the Ghost of Sue Ann McGee
The Girl Who Stirred up the Whirlwind
The Girl Who Motivated Murder Most Foul
The Girl Who Said Goodbye for the Last Time
Fall From Apocalypse
Armageddon Now
Worth
When Jesus Came to Jersey as the Son of Thunder
When Jesus Came to Canada to Lead an Indigenous Rebellion
Canadian Angels of Mercy – Nurses in Times of Peril
Points of Rebellion: Aboriginals Who Fought for Justice
Lynton Curls Her Hair
Lynton Buys a New Cell-Phone
and Hears the Voice of Doom
Lynton Walks on Water
Lynton and the Vampire at Tagaytay Manor
Chablis: Avenging Angel for the Forgotten
In the City of Lost Hope
Chablis and the Terrorist Who Resurrected the Spirit of Che

PURSUIT

TABLE OF CONTENTS

Introduction – 5
On the Verge of Catastrophe
Prologue – 7
A Web of Deceit and Murder
Chapter 1 – 13
Calm Was About to Crumble
Chapter 2 – 39
The Plot Thickens
Chapter 3 – 63
The Most Valuable Metal
Chapter 4 – 77
A Whirlpool of Mischief
Chapter 5 – 91
It is the Way We are Programmed
Chapter 6 – 123
Answer Wretches, Dying, Dying
Chapter 7 – 141
What We are Fighting to Achieve
Chapter 8 – 171
Only Slightly Better
Chapter 9 – 197
The Most Fearful Terror Group
Chapter 10 – 211
Only Problem is Which One
Chapter 11 – 234
Fight for the Soul of a Nation
Chapter 12 – 258
Devil's Calling Card In Mac's Hand
Chapter 13 – 285
Would They or Wouldn't They?
Epilogue - 297

J. Wayne Frye

PURSUIT

TO: Gay, who was an important part of my life
for a brief time and brought great joy to me
as we shared grand interludes of euphoria.
And, of course, to my muse – Lynton.

Catalogue Number: 8341-945-843

ISBN: 978-1-928183-09-9

Fireside Books – Victoria, British Columbia
Peninsula Publishing Consortium

J. Wayne Frye   4

PURSUIT

INTRODUCTION
ON THE VERGE OF CATASTROPHE

On a desolate, lonely island in the Pacific, a lone figure made its way to a cave where a dark secret had been harboured for almost 200 years. There was an object in the cave that possessed infinite power. The man carefully removed it from the cave and brought it into his home on the far side of the island.

Up until that time, the object had never been removed from the cave, and the 49 people who called the island home had lived a peaceful, quiet life free from the evils of the outside world. At one time the people had known greed, envy and hostility, but when a wise person sealed this object away in the cave, all that ended. Now, the object that came from far, far away long, long ago was brought into the light of day, and things changed on the island, changed for the worse when an older woman brought forth charges of abuse when she was a 15 year old against most of the men on the island. An ill-wind of evil had begun to blow across this tiny, barren outpost in the vast Pacific Ocean.

There was another man who went to work every day in a deep, dark cave in Langley, Virginia. He was an intelligence analyst for the C.I.A. who spent the day listening for unusual radio signals emanating from all over the world. His job was to

J. Wayne Frye   5

make sure that a paranoid nation was kept safe from any insidious intentions of those who might want to rain down another 9/11. He noticed an unusual signal coming from a tiny island in the South Pacific and immediately reported it to his superiors. He was not a field operative, but his superiors decided to send him there to investigate, and what he found instilled a fear that so overwhelmed him that when he returned to the USA he disappeared into the bowels of Manhattan, which was now a city on the verge of catastrophe.

PURSUIT

PROLOGUE
A WEB OF DECEIT AND MURDER

O.K., some people would call her a whore; others even went so far as to call her an aberration of nature. Whore? Well, that would depend on your definition. Real whores are not just women, but any entity that sells its soul for profit. Corporations, especially banks, come to my mind as the very apex of whoredom. In fact, I have much more admiration for streetwalkers than for banks. Streetwalkers are giving men a service that is straight-forward with no small type to hide insidious intentions. A whore is providing a commodity that brings satisfaction; although, it may only be transitory in nature. On the other hand, corporations bring very little real satisfaction and serve no valuable purpose other than as nefarious enterprises dedicated to the enslavement of mankind to consumerism on one-hand and to slavery as underpaid, under-appreciated workers on the other. Corporations represent the embodiment of a new feudal system with CEO's as the Lords of the Manor, and the workers and consumers as the current-day serfs.

So, was Chablis Louise Chavez (pronounced Sha-blee) a whore? One might consider dinner and a movie followed by sex as a form of prostitution if careful, thoughtful reflection manifested itself. After all, most women reward men for an evening of frivolity with a sexual peccadillo to top the

J. Wayne Frye   7

evening off. As I always asked women friends who would degrade streetwalkers, "Do you reward a man with sex when he spends money taking you out for an evening? If so, then how are you different from a streetwalker? After all, you are getting compensation in the form of things as opposed to money. Be very careful when you judge people."

Now, this is not a book of philosophical ramblings, so we shall not debate the merits of my contentions that being a whore is relative to the way one perceives things, but suffice it to say that Chablis Louise Chavez was a woman who simply made no apologies for enjoying sex. After all, she was an incredibly beautiful woman who was not judgemental of anyone but those who were themselves judgemental. You see, she knew first hand what it was to be ridiculed, belittled and judged by people. Chablis was a transsexual.

Unfortunately, the world is a place where religion is used to criticize and abuse rather than lift and praise, so she had endured finger pointing by self-righteous hypocrites in the little Mexican village where she was raised, and even in the more hedonistic environs of New York City she was often ostracized by so-called polite society. Still, this was a woman who simply refused to bend before the winds of adversity. So determined that she was often referred to as the Manhattan Mad Hatter of Hostile Indignation, she never allowed anyone to demean her without paying a heavy price.

Her date with Mac McAllister had gone well, and there would be no surprises, because she had told him beforehand that she had a very severe birth defect that might affect their relationship. Looking at her, Mac shook his head and said, "What birth defect?"

Chablis smiled and replied, "One that you cannot see until I undress. I am a pre-op transsexual. So, you see, I have the wrong genitals?"

Slightly taken aback, Mac, an educated man, understood the term gender dysphasia, but he had never, knowingly at least until this very moment, been around a transgendered person. To his credit, he said, "Well, I don't know how I will act if we decide to have sex, Chablis, if I should be so lucky, but I know that you are more woman than any woman I have ever known. So, let's see how things go. Frankly, there is one thing I will never be able to do, though. I hope you can understand that. If so, then I see no reason not to move forward with our date."

Chablis, with a little giggle, replied, "Well, I have never been one to force a man into doing anything he did not want to do. I promise to be gentle with you."

PURSUIT

The evening had gone well, but there was a bit of tension, as Mac was kissing her while they were in an erotic embrace. Feeling her natural, but hormonally assisted perky little breasts brought an intense erection to Mac, and he longed to undress her, but did not want to seem too pushy. Sensing his trepidation, Chablis got up and took his hand, gently pulling him toward the bedroom.

Standing at the foot of the bed, she gave him the full view of her 5:3 magnificently formed body as she slowly removed her dress, pulling it over her head to expose her braless, perky little breasts. All she had on were her high heels and very small panties. Mac stared down intently at her panties.

"I know how to tuck it in well, Mac. It is OK to be curious. It is natural."

"I, I…" stuttered a dumbfounded Mac.

Chablis, who had been through this with many men before, said, "Relax, I will leave them on for now. They don't even have to come off if you don't want me to take them off."

Undressing, Mac, as he pulled off his briefs, indicated by the extreme stiffness of his member that not much about Chablis was bothering him. Still, she had not removed her panties, but that was only a formality, as Mac immediately lay on top of her and began to kiss, lick and meander his way down toward her crotch, and as he did, he very artfully pulled her panties down to see that Chablis was not very well-endowed, so there was not much there to ponder. Mac simply put his hands behind her hips and very tactfully turned her over.

Now Chablis was meticulous in the way she kept herself clean, perfumed and well-prepared for giving men what they wanted from a woman of infinite allure. She spread her legs, reached up, grabbed the pillow and put it under her hips, boosting her magnificent ass high into the air where Mac could longingly gaze upon that opening that was, from years of use, wide open and ready for action. He kissed it lightly, and then flicked out his tongue, moistening it for what he knew would be divine penetration that would make them both soar to great heights of erotic blissfulness. Strangely, so intent was he on the magnificent display of womanhood that was in his face, he had no thoughts whatsoever of what was between the front of her legs, even though he had a glimpse of her balls that were hanging low in easy view. He was buried between magnificent cheeks that made him want to spend eternity worshipping them, just savouring the delight of what was the most incredibly soft flesh he had ever encountered. This was not just a woman. This was a goddess to be worshipped and adored.

Chablis whispered, "Give it to me, baby."

PURSUIT

Mac raised himself to his knees and gently placed the head of his stiff member into the huge opening. Chablis, skilled at relaxing her muscles, made it so incredibly easy for Mac that his member slid in like a well-oiled piston working up and down in the chamber of a hot engine. He was firing on all cylinders.

Each forward thrust was met enthusiastically by a steady backward thrust and a rapid squeezing contraction of her sphincter muscle as Chablis moaned with delight. She began to shout, "Harder, harder, faster, faster. Give it to me baby. Give it to me. Fill me up with your liquid love!"

The pounding got faster and more furious until they were both making guttural sounds, quickly moving toward that crescendo of release that would flood their minds, bodies and souls with ecstatic erotic euphoria. The climax came for both of them like a tsunami roaring ashore on some distant, deserted island – a wave of wantonness that rattled their souls as they both let out shouts of glorious satisfaction.

Mac crawled off and lay beside her. Chablis was still on her stomach, feeling his joy juice sink deeper and deeper into her anal cavity. Oh, if only this moment could last forever, but it couldn't, because lurking about in the city were killers, killers waiting to drag Chablis into a web of deceit and murder.

PURSUIT

CHAPTER 1
CALM WAS ABOUT TO CRUMBLE

Things had been looking very bleak for Chablis of late, as she and her partner, Aaron Adams, had been on a long dry spell of interesting cases. They both craved excitement and adventure, but the past year had been filled with boring divorce cases, an occasional tail job and some security details.

New York City was a place for pessimists unless you were part of the privileged class. The cost of living soared, but those at the top just kept making more and more while those at the bottom fell further behind as the system refused to equalize things and make those at the top pay their fair share. The real people on welfare were the rich who were allowed to reap vast amounts of social assistance through a tax system that always favoured those at the top while taking from those in the middle to provide minimal welfare for the poor and lavish welfare for the rich.

Manhattan and the other boroughs were just part of a bloated, unwieldy city that had lost hope for all but the few. The labour movement, what there was left of it, had yielded to austerity measures and no longer offered any hope for working men and women who were simply fodder for the machinery of capitalism that ground people up a little more each day. Hope had been sacrificed so the wealthy could enjoy the good life.

J. Wayne Frye

PURSUIT

The city was once a colossus of hope, but now it was like the rest of America, just another sacrificial lamb laid before the privileged class to be trampled on in service to their avarice disregard for humanity in the pursuit of more and more. Each day, the ranks of the poor grew while the rich garnered an ever greater percentage of the wealth. This was capitalism American style, and it was unrestrained by a government that was itself run by greedy politicians who rewarded themselves with lavish salaries and parsimonious benefits.

Social problems were intensified by a partisan divided federal government with sanctimonious hypocritical Republicans always siding against the poor, while Democrats, knowing they could not muster enough votes to change things, fanned the fires of sanctified indignation while secretly siding with the moneyed class, as they themselves were part of that class.

Social problems grew more pronounced each day while the rulers kept ballyhooing the grand democracy that was America. The media played along with this farce, and fanned the fires of war which kept the people occupied with the false notion that there was always some terrorist group, some other country out there that wanted to do America in, destroy the so-called democracy that was supposedly the envy of the world. Of course, the American people were too stupid to understand very few nations envied America, rather they deplored it.

Bad times were not just coming but were the daily reality of the middle class, and this was due to a government that was not meant to work for the benefit of the middle class and poor. Repressive laws were commonplace as those in power feared that one day the people might actually wake up to the manipulation that was keeping them in bondage.

Chablis and Aaron were avid socialists, but in America, that word had been made into something evil and fearful. Furthermore, the word liberal signified some hedonistic wild-eye anarchist who wanted to take money from the middle class and rich and give it to those lazy, good-for-nothing welfare loving poor who were such a drain on the system.

It is said that the only time real reform can take place is when there are so many poor that finally when they have absolutely nothing to eat they will decide to dine on the rich. However, the poor in America were also religious slaves, and they constantly fell for the idea that their reward would come after death when they all pranced through the streets of heaven that were lined with gold. Yeah, thought Chablis, keep the poor suckers believing in a glorious after-life, so they won't demand anything in this life.

PURSUIT

Chablis had heard so often from social reformers that the key was evolution not revolution. However, Chablis and Aaron both believed that you accomplished nothing by meekness. You get slapped on your right cheek and turn your left cheek, in the world of capitalism; the barons of greed will simply slap the left cheek also. Thus is the way of capitalism.

Of the absoluteness of this truth, Chablis was firmly convinced. What America needed was the nationalization of the means of production and distribution in the interests of a vast population that was being left behind. This was the only way to ameliorate an untenable situation. And how were the details of this vast change to be grappled with amid the throes of revolution? Only if streets were slippery with blood, the vilest passions unchained, stores, factories, and workshops wrecked, and a starving populace in revolt could the sanctification of mankind be revealed. Mankind could beat out a workable constitution in the turmoil. By all means, Chablis thought, have a revolution if a revolution is both a necessary and safe prelude to reform. But was it possible in a complacent, easily manipulated society like America? Could people who were propagandized into believing they lived in the greatest land on earth muster the intelligence and courage to see through the façade of lies that kept them in bondage to an ideal that simply did not exist? Oh holy lie, liberty was empty and without a heart.

PURSUIT

Chablis was well-known for her generosity and kind spirit. Though she often endured ridicule, particularly from those who deemed themselves religious paragons of virtue, she was well-respected and even venerated by many. One thing you always got from her – honesty. She pulled no punches and you always knew where you stood. Treat her with respect – you got the same. Show her disrespect, and you would often live to regret it.

She was taking a leisurely stroll down Broadway in the late afternoon, enjoying the nice weather in good disposition. However, her favourable disposition was about to receive short shrift. A cloud slipped over the sun, then another and another and suddenly the fog began to roll in from the Hudson River and shroud the buildings in a light mist. Now it was a raw dismal afternoon, the grim fog-robed buildings, the dripping vehicles, and the dusky pedestrians all about reminding her forcibly of the dread of evil that too often hung over the city. That feeling something was amiss floated slowly across her mind, and the gathering shadows around seemed fraught with a gentle melancholia. She made her way into Starbucks, ordered a latté, drew up a chair to the window and abandoned herself wholly to thought. What her meditations were matters very little, but what counts is that she felt a smart blow on her left shoulder and a voice said, "Damn, Chablis Louise Chavez, the wanton woman who is the heartthrob that titillates men's libidos like a swizzle stick in a Margarita filled with foamy passion."

Chablis looked up with a laugh as a stalwart individual with a thick black beard and singularly resolute face had broken upon her solitude. The acquaintance was none other than Roy Blount, journalist, who was a devoted disciple of Che Guevara. He was a dying breed, not only in America, but in the world. He was a died-in-the-wool hardcore communist. No law, no force, no reference of all social energies to voluntary association of individuals were his substitutes for the all-consuming die-hard socialism in which he fervently believed. He advocated waging all-out war in every effective mode, violent or otherwise, against the existing social system. He had been fired from some of the most prominent publications in the USA because of his fire-brand politics that simply demanded a violent upheaval of the social order and the complete annihilation of the privileged class before a firing squad. Even most left-wing publications considered him to hot to handle.

He was a free-lancer now, working for whatever news organization would pay him for his stories. Like all people in America who were true to their social convictions and defended the downtrodden, he had paid a high price for standing with the working men and women of a country that simply did not give a damn about the working class. This was a man who refused to bow before sanctimonious self-righteous hypocrisy, and stood like a grand beacon shining a light of devotion to a cause that had died long ago when the Berlin Wall tumbled and along with it destroyed any hope that capitalism might be defeated. Ronald Reagan's society of greed had won out by spending the nation into near bankruptcy building up the military to fight an enemy that had been largely a figment of the West's imagination. But what mattered was the capitalists had triumphed and stood victorious with all of humanity now laid bare before them for exploitation.

Though not as strong an advocate as Roy, Chablis was attracted to him for his political beliefs and for his gratifyingly handsome demeanour that titillated her libido. He talked of violence, but, so far as she knew, his hands had never been stained with any actual act of violence. Further, he was most sincere, resolute, and unflinching in his devotion to a cause in which he fervently believed, and he had, moreover, once saved Chablis from certain death when he stepped between her and a man who had pulled a knife on her. He took a stab wound to the stomach for her, and survived to remind her that he would accept payment for his brave deed in the form of sexual favours. She laughed about it with great vigour, but he seemed dead serious. Still, she had never repaid him with said favours, but had considered it many times.

PURSUIT

He told Chablis that there were rumours flying about terrorists who had infiltrated the nation without detection, and were planning the most violent act imaginable. The national government was keeping it quiet to quell any alarm on the part of the citizens, but they had determined that Roy might be aiding and abetting them since the government also considered him a security risk because of his die-hard communism and support of radical causes. Furthermore, his friends were also being watched, so he suggested at that very moment they may be under surveillance.

Chablis, as always, unabashedly defiant of any entity that might try to squelch her or any other American's freedom, said, "Fuck the U.S. government. I have about as much use for my government as I do for a those fascist assholes who started all this trouble with the invasion of Iraq to go after weapons of mass destruction that they knew did not exist. When they put those assholes in jail where they belong, then I may consider respecting the government. Until then, I stand defiantly alongside people like you who refuse to bow before the tyranny of the ruling class. Of course, you have been conspicuously absent from my life of late. What has kept you away for so long?

"I am a man with a mission, Chablis. My mission sometimes precludes me from socializing, but I do remember you owe me!"

PURSUIT

Chablis knew what he was talking about and let a smile creep across her face. "Well, I have not forgotten, but I am afraid of what you have between your legs. It might be more than I can handle."

"Never know until you try little girl."

Still smiling, Chablis replied, "True, but I know you anarchists are rumoured to have members as big as your egos."

Moving on, Roy said, referring to one of Chablis' most famous cases, "So, what are you and Aaron up to these days? Any cases like the Spirit of Che Guevara killer on your plate? If not, I have something I want to share with you."

Chablis replied, "My dear fellow, you choose your time oddly. I am taking a vacation back to Mexico in a few days, but at least tell me about what is on your mind."

"You can't stay a couple of days longer, can you? Say yes, and I will open your eyes to something interesting. It is worthwhile sometimes to take a good long hard look at things that might seem normal, but are, in fact, just the opposite."

Chablis sighed and replied, "If it is about the coming revolution, forget it. It is over Roy, the capitalists have won."

PURSUIT

"I think I have heard that remark before," Roy somewhat coldly rejoined, "still, say what you like, you will find that the reins of revolution may be passing to new hands and there is a stirring among the growing ranks of the poor who are weary of serving the privileged class."

Chablis, never one to mince words, replied, "There is a practicality to anarchism, but Americans are not very practical people. They are too easily manipulated by patriotic propaganda and, of course, by their professed love of Jesus, whom we all know is on America's side. People who truly believe in equality of opportunity are only a hand full, and politically speaking of no account, as our power is trumped by corporations and the wealthy, who are the ones truly served by the government. Forgive my bluntness, but to my mind, your crusade to free the masses simply falls on death ears at the top where government simply does not care and at the bottom where people are too wrapped up in mundane things like what the latest media whores on reality shows are doing to really care about things that truly matter. The world is run by morons who are nothing but stooges for the wealthy and corporations and the people keep voting against their own self-interests. Nothing is going to change, because this frankly is a nation of idiots who simply line up for their shackles and chains. People really want to be enslaved, because they don't want to think for themselves. They want others to do it for them."

PURSUIT

"As you like," said Roy doggedly; "the world has had enough barking. The time for biting has come. Restrain your eloquence for awhile, and I promise you a wonderful change of convictions. Come on Chablis; take a ride on the wild side with me."

"What have you and your anarchist friends got on your minds? Talk is cheap. As Charles O. Finley used to say, money talks and bullshit walks. OK, so, in your case it is action talks, bullshit walks. All I have ever seen from people who want change is talk and no action, because frankly, the people don't care. They just accept their lot in life without protest. You don't get change by going to you oppressors and begging for justice. You demand it! Americans are too complacent to demand change. That is why people like you and your anarchist friends are pariahs in the public mind. They cannot see that you need violent revolution to change things. Where do you think the African- Americans would be today if they had simply followed Martin Luther King on his peaceful marches begging for justice? It took a group of anarchists who started burning down the cities to make the government sit up and take notice. Only when the fires were consuming the ghettos and the rich and powerful started fearing their gated enclaves might be next did the government finally throw the African-Americans a bone to keep them at bay for awhile. That fire in the belly is gone now. It has played out."

PURSUIT

"I agree with you to a certain extent, Chablis. Compliancy and supplication converts no one, and strengthens the hands of the reactionaries, and, what is more, destroys useful capital. Why, the do-gooders say, injure society thus aimlessly? I say curse society! I detest both society as it is and society as most hope it will be. Today the capitalist wolves and the manipulated multitudes deserve each other. No one is standing against the culture of greed. Rather, it is aggrandized and praised. But about our numbers, my friend, you think that we must be politically impotent because we are relatively few in number. We may be only a few thousand, but we are devoted, dedicated to the betterment of mankind. Obviously I could hardly venture to bother you, but our people have some incalculable force behind them. Suppose, for instance, that the leaders of these few thousands came to possess some novel invention, something that made them invincible?" Looking very hard at her, he seemed almost coy, as if he knew some great and grand secret.

"Your coyness, your bombastic cockiness about this has piqued my interest, but I believe you are embellishing, using fiction to titillate my interest. Besides, I see no scope, even for such an invention, no matter how game-changing it might be. It is just another in a long line of utopian dreams fuelled by your genuine, but ill-conceived notion that the people of this country are actually interested in revolt. They are not! They are far too complacent, too wrapped up in the mundane to really care."

Very contemplatively, Roy said, "You remember Don Hart?"

"Now there's a typical case of genius wasted on anarchy. A pretty story is that of your last martyr. He tries to blow up a visiting prince and destroys a woman and her food cart on lower Park Avenue. That really endeared everyone to the cause, killing one of the people you want to help while the prince doesn't even take notice of the explosion as he is too busy waving at the adoring masses who worship at the alter of royal leeches who think they are special by virtue of birth."

"All men make blunders," growled the intrepid journalist. "That was ten long years ago. He was a very young man. But mark me, my friend, don't call people martyrs prematurely. You think Hart was killed when he was supposedly shot as he dived off the GW Bridge. I have my doubts."

"You don't think he is dead? As far as I know no one has ever survived a jump of the George Washington Bridge. That is like dropping a water melon from the Empire State Building onto the pavement. At that distance and at the speed a body falls, a dive off the GW is simply not survivable. The guy died. Just because no body was found doesn't mean he survived."

PURSUIT

Roy nodded enthusiastically and the dour look on his face indicated he was smug and assured about his contention. Chablis reflected back on when that mishap occurred. She was still in university in Mexico City, just preparing to graduate and head north to New York City to hook up as a partner with the man she had unabashedly admired, Aaron Adams. At that time, the USA was still reeling from 9/11 paranoia. It would never let go of its self-righteous indignation.

You would have thought it was the only nation to ever suffer a terrorist attack. The Americans were too stupid to realize that bin Laden had actually won, because he had struck such fear into the country that the people had willingly sacrificed what little freedom they had to be safe from those awful terrorists that had actually been manufactured by America in the first place. Bin Laden was backed by the CIA when the Soviet Union was the country the USA feared. There always had to be some evil entity out there to use to keep the people cowering in fear that someone was out to destroy the freedom they thought they had.

.

As for Hart's crime, Chablis considered it stale news if news at all. Suffice it to mention the attempt of this enthusiastic anarchist to blow up the Prince of Wales, or as Chablis called him, the Royal Leach of perpetual hereditary arrogance, was a colossal failure.

PURSUIT

Don Hart's malfeasance had made him a laughing stock among the revolutionary set, and what idiot would actually head across the GW Bridge knowing he was being pursued by New York's Finest on one side and by the New Jersey Highway Patrol on the other. Trapped on the bridge, he simply climbed up on the girder and in an act of desperation dived into the icy waters of the Hudson River. The swift current was assumed to have carried the body out to sea, and now Roy was actually suggesting that he survived. Doubtful thought Chablis.

The plot had been conceived in Saudi Arabia, the true home of most terrorist organizations, but one country never invaded by trigger happy America, because it simply had too much oil wealth and too much power. Anyway, it was the Saudis who had bailed George Bush II out of many failed business deals. He owed them. The entire Bush family owed them, and for that reason, Saudi diplomats were spirited out of the country immediately after 9/11 for fear the truth might be revealed. Hell, the truth meant nothing to the American public. They were so gullible they would believe anything the propagandists fed them. Almost 60% if the people actually believed Iraq was involved in 9/11. If gullibility was a virtue, the American people were the most virtuous people on the planet. Feed them a steady diet of patriotic propaganda sprinkled with a little bit of Jesus, and they would line up to die for a lie.

J. Wayne Frye

PURSUIT

After the assumed death of Don Hart, typical of American reaction, a wave of repression descended upon the nation and all across the globe U.S. aggressive actions was justified as necessary to protect the homeland. So, a bungled effort of an incompetent terrorist led to a tsunami of revenge that included using terrorism to fight terrorism. Now, that made a lot of sense, deplore the tactics of terrorists and then use those tactics to fight them. Granted, the terrorist had killed one innocent person, who paid the price for trying to make a buck by hawking some hotdogs while idiots were fawning over some royal asshole that never did anything worthwhile in his life.

Of course, there was the simultaneous destruction of a billboard displaying the golden arches. Now, maybe that was what really pissed Americans off. Hey, the Golden Arches and the exploited workers who serve you that hamburger with fries should not have been besmirched. After all, that is what America is all about – using the cheap labour of the masses to make the few rich.

Chablis had a sneer on her face, because as devoted as she was to righting the wrongs of a society based on greed, she could not accept the slaughter of innocents in the process. She knew that change required violent revolution not peaceful begging for justice. However, she could not countenance the slaughter of those who were the exploited in order to attack exploitation.

PURSUIT

The indignity of the authorities over what happened seemed to be concentrated more on the damage done to a billboard with the golden arches on it than with the hard working woman who fell victim to an anarchist who lacked the ability to carry out his intended aim. The irony was that had the anarchist succeeded in killing the Prince of Wales, the asshole would have just been replaced with the next royal leech in the succession line. There was no end to those who by virtue of birth were elevated to special status in a world that was supposed to be democratic. What was democratic about having royalty who never achieved anything and never contributed anything positive to mankind? Princess Diana was revered and idolized by so many, but what was she? Nothing but a royal whore who died in a $250,000 Mercedes with her rich boyfriend by her side as they sped away from those who wanted to photograph the rich and famous, so the peons could look with awe upon their idols. The world was sick with banality and Chablis saw no hope for change, as the masses were too complacent and the rich were too powerful.

"O.K." said Chablis rather of matter-of-factly. "So, what do you want from me? You think Don Hart is alive, and I suppose you think his so-called accomplice who planned the attack, Bobby Swift, who was supposed to have died at sea on a ship that sunk on its way to Holland, is also alive and kicking."

PURSUIT

"They both had huge revenues from bank robberies they had committed for nearly a year before the attack. With money, anything is possible. You know that."

"Hey, it has been ten years and no one has questioned the authenticity of what occurred. Anyway, you are on these guys side. Why would you want to find them, if they are alive? An anarchist loving journalist like you should be praising their escape from justice, not trying to hinder it."

"That is true Chablis, but first and foremost, I am a journalist. I want the truth. Who knows, maybe I could write a piece aggrandizing their escape from the rich-man's justice."

"What about the hotdog vender. Is she not entitled to justice? Why does she pay the price while that royal asshole goes on living a life of luxurious splendour on the backs of the middle class and poor who support his lavish lifestyle with their taxes?"

"You are right Chablis. There are many victims in this affair. I would add that among Swift's victims must, in a sense, be his mother. She has led a life of loneliness in the Bronx, doing charitable work in an attempt to atone for her son's misdeeds. She is a victim as much as anyone else is."

PURSUIT

"How do you know of her plight?"

"I know her very well indeed; although, she is never very pleased to see me when I visit. Still, I am on excellent terms with the old lady, but I have not seen her for some weeks now."

Roy rose from his chair, stood there staring down at Chablis and said, "Be sure and look me up early on your return from Mexico. Mischief, I tell you, is brewing and something stupendous is about to occur. There is a rumble in the streets where I keep close watch on what is happening."

He was moving to the door when Aaron Adams popped over with a note in his hand. Chablis knew he had been standing there for awhile behind a fish tank probably listening to the conversation. He glanced at her and winked as he said hello to Roy, dropped the envelope and said, "An invitation. Enjoy yourself. Good to see you Roy." He then turned and walked out.

Chablis got up and said, "Wait a minute Roy. I will walk out with you." As she was talking, she opened the envelope, which she knew Aaron had already read as it was not sealed, just had the flap inserted inside the seal part of the opening. Hey, that was Aaron. Being a private eye meant that you were naturally nosy and being in people's business just came natural. She took no offence to it.

PURSUIT

Yes, there was no mistaking the handwriting; the missive was from her friend, Lynton Viñas, who was in town from the Philippines. How wonderful thought Chablis. Lynton, like Chablis was a renowned investigator, only she investigated the supernatural. In fact, she was known in the Philippines as Lynton Viñas, demon fighter.

Chablis wondered if Lynton's boyfriend, Wayne, was with her. You see, Wayne was a writer and had written books about Chablis and Lynton's grand adventures. In fact, he had made them both relatively famous.

Lynton and Chablis had become great friends when she was in Manila on a case that dealt with a supposed Aswang (similar to a vampire) that was murdering young pregnant girls in a poor area of Metropolitan Manila. While doing so, they had made a good friend, and in Chablis' case, an intimate friend, of a well-known newspaper publisher, Donald Perez.

Only two weeks before, Chablis had talked to Donald, but as she read the note, she realized she would never talk to him again. Genial Donald, an agnostic in a country where being so was almost a crime, due to the control exercised by the Catholic Church, had died at the young age of 47. Poor Donald thought Chablis. He was such a vibrant, lively man who, though not very handsome, had certainly aroused great passion in Chablis.

PURSUIT

She read the note:

Dear Chablis,

"I have just arrived on business from Manila, where, I am afraid, something sad has occurred. Our friend, Donald Perez, died almost two weeks ago, leaving his friend Robert Hernandez, who lives in Queens, as one of his executors. As the estate is in rather a muddled condition, a good deal of attention may be necessary, so while I am here, his cousin asked me to lend any assistance I might be able to. I am staying at the Times Square Holiday Inn and would be delighted to see you.

With best wishes,

Lynton

P.S. Our friend Lena Langley gets $100,000, and you and I get $20,000 each. Can you imagine Don leaving us that much money, especially since I had no idea he was even mildly wealthy.

"Excuse me, Roy," Chablis said, turning to my neglected friend, "but this letter is most important. A nice business pickle I am in, I can tell you."

Smiling, as he got a whiff of the notepaper, Roy said, "What incredibly nicely-scented note-paper your business correspondents use. You have my deep sympathies. Well, farewell for the present."

PURSUIT

"Don't be in a hurry," Chablis said; "I am afraid I must postpone my Mexican trip after all. This note changes everything."

Blount stared, and concluded that something really serious was up. "So you will be available for two or three days longer. That being so, I shall expect to see you at the old place about eight o'clock tomorrow evening. Be sure and come, for I have a guest with me of peculiar interest to both of us."

Chablis was curious about who it was, but decided not to press the issue. She laughed heartily and thought what a chequered life she lived and what unusual friends she had. Her wonderful life was one of excitement and adventure, and though she did not know it at the time, she was about to undertake one of her most curious adventures.

Yes, she had been exposed to wild-eyed anarchists, avid communists, brazen blackmailers, hired killers, jihadists, thieves of all kinds, and worst of all, U.S. government agents and provocateurs who thought they had free rein to do as they pleased because they were defending liberty. Liberty, yeah, thought Chablis, what liberty?

She had been an avowed Marxist since childhood, when she had endured abject poverty in

PURSUIT

a Mexican village where one privileged family ruled like royalty and subjected everyone to slave-like conditions toiling for them so they could lead lives of luxurious splendour while their workers struggled to put food on their tables.

Chablis had embraced socialism, but frowned on the lukewarm embracing of it by those who were more talk than action. Still, she had long ago given up on any appreciable change, because she saw the poor as too wrapped up in religion and patriotic babble to do anything about their plight. As her friend Aaron Adams often said, "Ronald Reagan destroyed the working man when he nailed the lid shut on the coffin of unionism. And the public actually proclaimed him the greatest American. Yeah, great for the rich and corporations, but he was just an undertaker for working men and women."

Chablis believed in violent revolution, but who would take up arms against an all-powerful state that spared no amount of wrath when it came to the defence of the wealthy and privileged. The wage slaves were there to serve the privileged class and anyone brazen enough to defy authority had to be crushed. The jails were full of people who dared question authority. Again, as Aaron said, there was one brief time in the 1960's when real revolution was ready to unfold, but once the Vietnam War ended, revolutionary movements lost their purpose and fizzled out.

J. Wayne Frye

PURSUIT

Long ago, there were dedicated journalists who defied authority and laid bare the truth of what was happening, but today, there were no journalists, only pretty faces handing out pabulum to the masses to placate them and convince them of American righteousness. FOX NEWS was nothing more than a mouthpiece for conservative and religious causes that was to news what slop was to pigs. They fed the public garbage and called it news. Although FOX was the worst, other news programs were not much better.

The wage slaves had accepted their lot and by watching reality television actually believed that they had a shot at the good life, when the good life, was in reality, only reserved for the chosen few. Still, the myth of "everybody can make it in America" was promoted and ballyhooed by the media to convince those at the bottom that they had a chance.

Chablis was a realist, and she had never owned a television, because she refused to fall prey to the banality that passed as entertainment. Her friends Wayne, Lynton and Aaron had also eschewed television long ago out of self-respect, as they refused to be manipulated by mass media, and Chablis, over the years, had developed a reputation as a woman of infinite charm, beauty and above all, intelligence. She was admired by one and all as a woman who never wavered in the pursuit of justice.

PURSUIT

Chablis was not the orator her friends Wayne and Aaron were, but she was, like them, free of the constant pursuit of material gain for the sake of what one could accumulate, because within her heart beat the rhythm of compassion for the downtrodden who had to toil in obscurity so the few could get rich on their backs. She firmly believed that to have a rich class you had to have a working class that made it possible for those at the top to enjoy a life of lavishness. She deplored the rich, for the most part, and saw them as leeches that drained the life out of society.

That night, lighter visions were to beguile Chablis' thoughts. When she dwelt upon once more meeting dear Lynton, an angel of a woman, but still a dynamic dynamo of energy in a 5:2 frame that made her only one inch shorter than Chablis, she could not help but smile, as she knew Lynton to be the most fervent devotee of justice she had ever known. Still, that was tomorrow night when she would meet Lynton, so she needed rest to prepare for what she thought would be a pleasant interlude, but, in the end, what is pleasant can harbour ill-intents. Also, there was Roy Blount's admonition not to miss seeing him at the "usual place" as he called it. That was, indeed, a mystery of some magnitude, because Roy was a man with a purpose to everything he did. Nothing was random happenstance with him. The mention of that ancient anarchist attempt on the life of the Prince of Wales had a purpose. Yes, thought

PURSUIT

Chablis as she drifted off the sleep, the period of relative calm in her life was about to crumble.

CHAPTER 2
THE PLOT THICKENS

It was with a light heart that Chablis made her way to Lynton's. The prospect of a chat with the charming, intelligent Lynton was exciting, and when she saw her two friends Channa and Ingrid there, she was delighted. For those two were, like Lynton, beautiful young women with an unstinting devotion to justice and fair play.

Now, I have described Chablis many times in many books, and each time she seems to improve with age. The same can be said of Lynton Viñas, as she was a woman whose beauty became more pronounced with maturity. However, her beauty was much more sublime than Chablis'. With Chablis you got in-you-face sexuality that, when it came to men, often caused more erections than a skin flick on a big screen television featuring two women having sex with one another. The bulges in men's pants when she was around would keep a tailor busy replacing popped zippers for weeks. However, with Lynton, you got a subdued sensuality that started much higher than a man's crotch. Her beauty titillated the brain of men who saw a glow of angelic sweetness that started with the compassionate twinkle in her eyes and worked its way down to her flat Asian nose that seemed to slightly jut out from a dark brown face that was untouched by the skin whiteners so many Asian women used in an attempt to be white.

PURSUIT

Lynton was proud to be Asian and knew how to highlight her Asian features to perfection. Her thick, succulent, luscious, puffy, moist lips almost seemed to be begging for a kiss. Her perfectly symmetrical chin swept gracefully down to a thin neck that blended delightfully onto an upper chest that was so soft looking that one could imagine it was as light to the touch as the finest Belgium lace. Then, like a slap in the face to awaken you, her small, perky, perfectly-shaped breasts stuck out with a defiance that made men sigh with appreciation. They were not blatant objects of desire, but rather, soft manifestations of blissfulness that appeared to need fondling, kissing, sucking and worshipping as if you were a newborn baby getting the nourishment of life.

Below those magnificent orbs was a stomach, not muscular, but still as taunt as an archer's bow, as her tight fitting blouses or dresses seemed to hug it with affection. Below that was her most womanly feature of all, and when she had on slacks, the indentation between her legs made men swoon with thoughts of carnal delight that could only be satisfied by paying homage to her womanliness. And her legs, what a perfectly shaped monument to the Greek love goddesses of old. The thighs were perfection personified and the muscular calves let you know that she had been a dancer at one time, and made you fantasize about having her do a dance of love naked before you as you gratefully took in the grandeur of a

PURSUIT

perfect woman who exuded a disarming sweetness that made you swoon with admiration and appreciation.

Oh, and her absolute finest asset (how is that for a pun – asset). Yes, her gorgeous ass was like a Michelangelo work of art, the pièce de résistance that made her look as good going as coming. It was the most absolutely perfectly sculpted ass to every grace the earth. It was an incredible work of art that should have had its own special room at the Louvre in Paris, so that mankind could appreciate the finest ass to every walk on the planet. If there is a God and he sculpted Eve's ass, it would have been a distant second in beauty to that which gracefully wiggled from side to side as Lynton seemed to float rather than walk down the street. In fact, when she gracefully glided down the street, men would often bump into lampposts or lose their balance as they turned to gaze upon the sweet, gentle sway of the bouncy butt of desire that titillated and tormented all lucky enough to gaze upon it.

There, beside Lynton were her two best friends, Channa and Ingrid, two equally beautiful women. Channa had that sophisticated beauty that came from someone who was well-bred, well-educated and well-equipped with all the essentials that made a woman desirable. She usually wore big-rimmed glasses that exemplified an intelligent woman with precise diction that let you know this

J. Wayne Frye41

woman had more than just sensuality. This was a woman who had intelligence to compliment her beauty. She was tall for a Filipino and every centremetre was a monument to sexuality that could not be corralled or harnessed. However, she was not an easy woman, and expected men to work hard for her attention.

Ingrid, on the other hand, was a bit more outwardly sensual. Like Chablis, she made no attempt to hide her interest in men. Her manner was more direct and the twinkle in her eye let you know immediately when she had a prurient interest in you. Men fawned over her, and her tall, lithe frame was perfectly formed. Her long, dark, flowing hair fluttered about her shoulders and accentuated a perfectly shaped face that made men long to wrap her in their arms and taste the nectar from those succulent-looking lips that seemed to be pleading for a kiss.

The meeting took place in the banquet hall of the hotel, and there were many people around, as it was a formal affair to welcome Lynton, Channa and Ingrid to the Filipino Fraternal Society of New York City. Lynton introduced Chablis to some of the people and they gradually made their way over to a table where the four girls took seats and got caught up on the latest news, sharing what had happened to them all since their last meeting in Manila nearly a year ago. It was a glorious reunion filled with great merriment.

PURSUIT

As a rule, receptions of this sort were tedious for all the girls; prolific only of deep dyspepsia and boring conversations. Most of the people were upper middle class individuals trying to act like they were upper class. Ordinarily, all four girls would have avoided association with such an organization, but they explained to Chablis that they were forced into attending as their air fare and accommodations were paid for by the society. So to save money, they could force themselves to endure one night of tedious boredom among those who aspired to be part of the upper class.

With a cynical sneer, Ingrid said, "upper middle-class mediocrity is swarming about here, but these people are too wrapped up in aspirational stupidity to realize they would never be admitted to the upper class anyway." Then she laughed as she said, "They are all the wrong colour and from the wrong country."

They all laughed as Chablis added, "Hey, I am Mexican. That is almost as bad as being Filipino."

Then, Lynton offered, "Wait a minute, we can all make it in high society. After all, my dear Wayne has made us famous with his books. If you are famous, sometimes your skin colour and nationality are overlooked."

Channa said, "Wait a minute. Wayne's prose is not very flattering toward the upper class."

J. Wayne Frye   43

PURSUIT

Lynton, putting her right index finger to her lips whispered, "Hush, don't mention Wayne's name. He always says, let people know you are my friend, and that is an invitation to get thrown out of a place."

They all laughed, as they knew and appreciated Wayne's penchant for being irreverent.

Chablis always had great reverence for Lynton, as she knew her as the kindest, most unassuming person she had ever met. Now Lynton was a genuine celebrity, affectionately and lovingly known as "The Demon Fighter" in the Philippines, and her renown was fairly evident in America also, as Wayne's four books dealing with her adventures in the supernatural realm had been best sellers.

Most celebrities are overly impressed with themselves and are best avoided if one does not want to endure self-aggrandizement from them. Happily, Lynton was the exception, as she looked upon herself as nothing special. As the imbecilic social climbers kept coming by the greet her, Chablis marvelled at Lynton's patience and politeness. Then, Lena Langley, a woman of maybe 40, and the chief recipient of Donald's largesse, whom Chablis had originally met on board a ship in the Suez Canal where Chablis was on a case, came by to say hello. She was invited to sit and chat, as all there knew her and appreciated her company generally, although at times she could border on the obnoxious.

Her politics were not as liberal as the others at the table, but despite a conservative bent, all the girls could not help liking her. They all wondered why Donald had left the bulk of his estate to her. After all, he hardly knew her.

Chablis reflected on how she had met Lena three years before in the Suez. The promenade deck of a P. and O. steamer offers boundless facilities for forming friendships, and during the brief interval which bridged her trip down the Suez and her arrival in New York City, she was engaged in constant conversation by Lena, whom it seemed was showing a romantic interest in Chablis. Lena was on the boat with her father, who was taking one last trip before his impending death from a progressive form of cancer for which there was no cure. Chablis had never discounted romantic interludes with women, although she much preferred the company of men. Anyway, she was fearful that Lena might find her birth defect a deal-killer, as a non-operative transsexual did not have the sexual part that Lena was obviously most interested in. However, when she shared the information with her, there actually seemed to be a heightened interest on her part. Chablis, however, did not find herself romantically attracted to Lena, and let her know that nothing sexual would come of a friendship.

PURSUIT

It should be pointed out here that cordial relations set up between the two had never dampened and that the two had maintained contact, and even seen each other on occasion. Lena's two brothers had also been on the trip and; although they were serving in the military in another ridiculous American adventure in spreading democracy in the Middle East, the two were not antagonistic toward Chablis, even though they knew she was an avowed socialist and vehemently against American nation-building in far off places.

Ironically, Lena's father was also an avowed socialist, but felt his son's, being from the upper middle class, should not, like most of the non-poor, avoid service in the military. To him, it was a matter of honour that his children were not exempt from having to serve.

Chablis had shared several evenings discussing Marx with the elder Langley, and the two of them had great rapport. In fact, he had hinted that Chablis should make a dying old man happy with a flirtatious sexual interlude. She had laughed at him, but felt that he was indeed serious, and her good nature had actually made her contemplate making an old dying man happy. However, before anything could be arranged, he had taken ill and had to spend the entire trip in bed, heavily sedated to deaden the pain from the cancer that was reaching its zenith.

PURSUIT

Chablis got up, and said, "I need some fresh air."

She walked out to the terrace and was joined by Lena. She smiled at Chablis, reached down and took her hand. "Well, are we ever going to enjoy a romantic interlude?"

"Lena, if I was attracted to women, you would be the one I would choose, but alas, I am a die-hard heterosexual I fear."

"Well, I hope you don't mind my continuing to ask."

"Of course not, it is always nice to be found appealing."

Smiling and nodding thanks, Lena said, "Well, I hope you know my dear old dad would have loved to have had a rendezvous with you. He talked of you on his death bed you know. He said that you were his favourite Marxist after Lenin."

The two girls laughed, and Chablis did not reject Lena as she continued to gently squeeze her hand, holding it softly as the two gazed out at the city lights.

Lena took a deep breath and said, "You know Jim Laleer? He is planning on running for Congress."

PURSUIT

"Oh my, he lives in the only really conservative district in Mid-town Manhattan. He is far too moderate to satisfy those right wing Wall Street fascists. If you aren't rich, if you don't love Jesus, if you aren't a die hard flag-waving patriot, if aren't a Republican reactionary, you don't stand a snow ball's chance in hell of getting elected. Why is he wasting his time?"

"Well, the Republican, Bob Ramson is running for re-election, but he is not conservative enough for those tea-bag Nazis, so they are putting up an independent candidate of their own for the general election, so Jim thinks the general election will have those two splitting the conservative vote, which means he might squeak in."

"Good luck. I doubt there are more than a hand full of genuinely compassionate people in that district. Not even a condo there sells for less than three million. Those are the people who destroyed the economy and were allowed to laugh all the way to the bank as Obama basically pardoned them for all their crimes, just like he gave Bush and Cheney a pass on the war crimes. Promise and hope, like always, was laid bare before the barons of greed who trampled on that hope and promise like everything else that stands between them and the bank vaults where they store their ill-gotten gains while the rest of us pick up the tab for their malfeasance, and their lavish lifestyles that are an abomination."

PURSUIT

"You know," said Lena, "compassion and rich are two mutually exclusive terms in most cases, and the Republican Party has become as ugly as it can get on things, but just when you think it can't get any worse, somehow it does. Today, it is a very ugly party made up mostly of white men, Jesus loving hypocrites and, of course, rich tycoons who think we are all here to serve their needs. However, I am not sure that trouble is not brewing among the masses. I know that anyone who dares question authority is labelled a terrorist, but people are beginning to realize that terrorism is all the privileged class leaves those of us who are always on the outside looking in. Eventually, the poor are going to say they have had enough, and there are far more of us than there are of them. They can't kill us all."

Chablis turned to her as they still held hands, and said, "My, I never knew you were so passionate about the plight of the poor. However, dear Lena, I am afraid the poor have been defeated long ago, and they have not the stomach to fight any longer. They are too busy watching what some reality star is doing, puffing on cigarettes, drowning their misery in drugs and alcohol to get up off their sofas of despair and do something to change things. Probably the best invention for the privileged class is the television, as it provides diversion for the masses and twists their brains to mush so that the moneyed oligarchs can maintain complete control free of interference."

PURSUIT

Lena let go of her hand, put her arm around Chablis' shoulder and said, "I am not so sure. I hear rumblings among the anarchist set who know the government has them under surveillance and though they are fearful of being rounded up and locked up under that abomination, the Patriot Act, they seem unafraid and more determined than ever to try and bring about change. The reckless agitators among them seem to be getting the upper hand as the gulf widens between the haves and have-nots in this country more each day."

Suddenly, from behind them, a crackling, older voice uttered, "I agree with you young lady. There is only one answer left for the masses, and that is violent upheaval. It is the last resort for those who have no power and who have lost all hope. That buffoon Ronald Reagan sacrificed the middle class and the poor to the greedy Wall-Street bastards and the people, when they occasionally get a decent democrat as President, wind up tying his hands by electing Republicans to Congress who keep the President from doing anything positive. Now, that Obama was an abomination if you ask me. He caved in all the time, refusing to stand up for the little guy against those greedy bastards. I stand with the anarchists. Tear it all down, arrest those greedy bastards, line 'um against a wall like Che did and blow their goddamn brains out. While their brains are lying on the ground, bring in a bulldozer and crush their bones, bury them along with their arrogance and greediness."

PURSUIT

The two girls were taken aback by the forcefulness of the old gentleman, and he was not through as he continued. "Socialism is the answer for the ills of the middle class and poor in America. Look at the rest of the First World where healthcare for all is a right rather than a privilege like it is here in America. Revolution is the only hope in this country, because the government has been bought by the wealthy and corporations. I deplore violence, but is it not violent to make people work for slave wages? Is it not violent to allow nearly 20% of the children in America to live in poverty so a few at the top can dine on caviar? Is it not violent to force people on the streets when they lose their jobs? Is it not violent to deny decent welfare to the poor while giving lavish welfare to the rich and the corporations? We live in a feudal system worse than that the people endured during the Middle Ages. Capitalism is the most evil economic system ever invented. We are told it is the greatest system in the world and that greed is good, because it makes people want to succeed and gives us all cheap products and services. I say bull-shit. Today's capitalism is slavery of the masses to the few at the top."

Chablis and Lena, dumfounded at the tirade foisted on them by the little old man, could not help but chuckle. He looked disgustedly at them, threw up his hands and said, "Damn, see, nobody wants to hear the truth."

J. Wayne Frye   51

PURSUIT

Chablis, in a softly modulated voice to indicate her calm assessment of what he had said, replied, "Oh, we are sorry. We meant no disrespect. It is just so unusual to see a passionate anti-establishmentarian of your age. Most older people support the system of servitude called capitalism, because they have been propagandized into subservience to an ideal America that simply does not exist."

Emphatic in his response, he tilted his head and pumped his right arm as he said, "Damn right girl. Damn right! Now you are talking my language. I never swallowed the goddamn propaganda, never. I got a brain, and I know how to use it. Most Americans are too busy loving Jesus, too busy watching sports on television, too busy buying things they can't afford to stop and really think how they are being manipulated."

"Unfortunately," said Chablis, "most people are just as you describe. It takes effort to change things, and most people gave up long ago, because things never change. What we need is a parallel government that represents the people with our own ready-made constitution and brand-new panaceas for suffering. We need to ignore the authority that represents the moneyed class and work for the betterment of all. Maybe the police would even begin to stop harassing the people and supporting the wealthy, and come over to the side of fairness and justice."

PURSUIT

The old man said, "I am Justin Hartman, and I am an old-time rebel rousing anti-authoritarian son-of-a-bitch." He then pointed at Chablis and said, "You I know, Chablis. You and Aaron Adams are always fighting for the little guy." Then, turning to Lena, he continued, "You, I don't know, but I like what you say."

"I am Lena Langley. Pleased to meet you Mr. Hartman."

"Justin please, Mr. Hartman makes me feel so old."

Lena smiled, nodded her head and said, "Being a liberal at your age is indeed unusual."

"Liberal is the key word for those of us who recognize that unfettered greed is the real anarchy in the world today. Unfettered capitalism in America has led to an oligarchy."

Chablis leaned against the terrace railing and said, "Barrack Obama came from humble beginnings, but rose to the most powerful position in the world, but he forgot those humble beginnings and bowed to those in Congress and the business community who refused to allow some semblance of fairness into the system. He let Bush and Cheney get away with war crimes, let the Wall Street tycoons walk away with billions and handed the insurance companies exactly what they wanted – more customers. It is time we made demands on the capitalists, stopped allowing them to pollute with impunity. It is time we put a stop to banks being allowed to lose our money and then be bailed out by the government, the same government that tells us when we need help that we are on our own. It is time we stopped allowing the Republicans to curtail the voting rights of minorities. It is time we demanded that the government work for us, not for the rich and the corporations."

Chablis continued, "Corporations accomplish nothing without government help, even if it is only tax incentives. The great engineering feats are ballyhooed as accomplishments capitalism made possible, but the truth is the government gave capitalists incentives or they would never have taken the risks. There is no debating that the country is made better by corporations and the things they can accomplish, but it is also made better by government. Despite what the Republicans say, government bureaucrats are invaluable. Why shouldn't they make sure your workplaces are safe? Would corporations make the workplace safe if there was no government regulation? No, higher profits are more important than human life to the greedy corporations. So, while liberals are creating the conditions for clean water, a clean environment, saving endangered species and seeing that everyone has the right to vote, the conservatives cry get the government out of our lives, when what they really mean is let the corporations destroy the environment and sacrifice our lives all in the name of profit. I defy anyone to list one positive thing a conservative has done for America. There are none, because all they do is worship Jesus and corporations. Both are used as control mechanisms to keep the poor in bondage."

The old gentleman shook his head, smiled sheepishly, and said, "Damn girl. You can be an agitated bitch. I read Frye's book about the anarchist who called himself the Spirit of Che Guevara. I know you admire Che and are the best damn private eye in New York City. You got your priorities in order."

Chablis, seeing Lynton standing in the far corner, listening with Channa and Ingrid to the conversation, said, "Meet my friends from the Philippines." As they exchanged pleasantries, Chablis continued with glee her rhetorical rambunctiousness. "The workers of this nation will hopefully one day rebel and take to the streets to demand justice. I hope that complacency will one day die out, and that the workers will begin to realize that they have to take their own destinies in their hands." Chablis suddenly remembered who Hartman was and blurted out, "Hartman, Hartman yes. You are the one who conspired to blow up the Queensboro Bridge a few years ago. You old anarchist you, when did you get out of jail? I thought they threw away the key on you, locked you up as an example of what happens if you even dare to advocate the use of violence to bring about change in a nation that considers change a threat to the social order. The USA can go all over the world and violently bring about regime change, but any attempt at regime change in this country gets you thrown in the slammer."

Winking at her, Hartman replied, "Well, I have been diagnosed with terminal cancer, so the current government showed some compassion. Damn unusual for the U.S. government to do that, uh? The irony is there are real anarchists on the loose and headed back here to do some real damage."

Chablis did not hesitate. She knew immediately who it was. "Don Hart and Bob Swift?"

Again, smiling, he said, "Bingo girlie. They are right when they say you are one smart cookie. Truth is neither one of them died the way the government figured they did. The government needed them dead to take the heat off the FBI for flubbing the whole deal. Now those two boys ain't your usual Islamic terrorists we are all supposed to be so fearful of. These boys are real home-grown Americans ready to blast away at what they see as the hypocritical American empire." Hartman puffed out his chest a bit and got a smug look on his face as he continued. "These boys are well-armed and ready to do some real business."

PURSUIT

"Why are you telling me all this?" said Chablis.

"Because I know all about you. You are as much a revolutionary as anybody who ever revered Che Guevara, but you also are a woman who sees unmitigated disregard for human life as evil and wants to protect the innocent. You hate unrestrained evil whether it is from the government or from anarchists who think taking innocent lives is just collateral damage in the process of building a just world. That makes them no better than the government they want to bring down. The USA wound up being no better than the terrorists when they used terrorism to fight terrorism. Bush and Cheney destroyed any moral high ground the USA initially enjoyed by becoming terrorists themselves. So, I know you will not try to kill Hart and Swift, but rather temper their propensity for killing innocents in the process of attacking the evil of a nation that must one day be brought to heel for its hypocritical arrogance and self-righteousness."

For some reason, at this point, a pensive looking Lena said, "Goodbye" and sailed off into the banquet room.

Curious, the demure dynamo, Lynton Viñas, walked over to the old gentleman and eyed him almost pityingly. He grinned at her and said, "Do not pity me little lady. I see in your eyes that you think me a foolish old man who is ranting idiocies, but mark my words. Great trials are coming as sure as the sun will rise tomorrow."

He then turned and left as Lynton, Chablis, Ingrid and Channa all looked at one another quizzically. They walked back into the banquet hall. The ordeal over, Chablis sat back down beside Lena for a tête-à-tête discussing what had just occurred. She let Chablis know that she was not totally ignorant of politics, but found the current state of affairs in the USA simply too deplorable to waste time since it was simply beyond hope of change. The old man and the two supposed terrorists now plotting some abominable act were all no worse than the government that allowed the corporations and wealthy carte-blanche when it came to what they desired. She reached under the table, took Chablis hand, bent over and whispered, "I just wish you and I could find a quiet desert island where we could make love all day and forget the world's problems. I am so sick of terrorism alerts, political chicanery, mundane musings about what the rich and famous are doing, ridiculous fascination with religious prophecy and how Jesus is going to swoop down from heaven and save all who are righteous from the coming apocalypse. The world is an awful place because of corporations, greed, American militarism and a complete lack of compassion for the common man. I say to hell with it all, let's just you and I go somewhere nice and fuck our brains out."

PURSUIT

"I wish it was that easy Lena. How I wish first I could forget my heterosexuality and then second turn my back on the coming misery, but I can't."

It was at this point that Lena mentioned Robert Hernandez to whose home they had both been on occasion. "You know Robert has been a widower for awhile now, and I fear his loneliness is beginning to overwhelm him. We will all have to visit him soon for the dispensation of Donald's will."

Chablis was interested in the topic, as she was anxious to know about the old man's welfare. "Is he in good spirits now that he has perhaps come to grips with the fact his son's body will never be brought down from that infernal mountain that has claimed so many lives?"

"He has I think. That was an ill-fated expedition that is now a part of the lore of Mount Everest. It has been almost ten years, so the time has helped heal the wounds from the loss. Robert once told me that it gave him great solace that his wife had died before his son's untimely death, as it would have been so unbearable for her since she doted on him so."

"Yes, he has endured great pain with her slow and agonizing death from cancer, and then losing his son shortly afterward must have been a blow that nearly ended him."

J. Wayne Frye   59

PURSUIT

Lena let go of Chablis' hand, as Lynton and her charges listened to the two as they exchanged information on Hernandez, whom they all knew.

Lena said, "The last time I saw him he was in marvellously good spirits and he never mentioned his wife or son, not once. We both know the son was a bit of a rogue who supported radical causes, but still, I suppose, love is blind."

"Yes, he was such a spoiled child, spoiled adult, too. They both tried to satisfy his every whim. Why when he went to Yale to study engineering, he was too good to stay in a dormitory or even a modest apartment. They bought him a 4000 square foot mansion in New Haven. Still, one cannot deny his intellectual vigour. He was a smart boy with a brilliant career predicted. Then, he meets that odd creature from the Philippines, a miscreant if ever there was one. That man gradually inspired him with a hatred toward his own mother and father after they had pampered and spoiled him. He sacrificed to his aim, position, comfort, reputation, his studies, everything to embrace this man as a lover, a guide through life. They moved into a loft in Soho and lived a bohemian lifestyle, which was frankly admirable, considering he wealth of Jack Hernandez's parents. Yet, did he not owe his parents at least a modicum of respect? Frankly, turning his back on wealth inspired me and made me in awe of him, but is there a necessity to revile your parents, as he did?"

PURSUIT

Quizzically, Lynton piped in, "Whatever happened to Jack's lover? I remember a letter he once had composed to the people of the Philippines before he moved to America saying that minds should be fired against governments that oppress and that those governments should be toppled by righteous indignation. It was absurd, he held, for a few men to possess all the wealth and that he trusted that one day the capitalist governments of the world would lie in ruins. He was actually a very eloquent man. Strange though, no one ever saw him, it was as if he was a ghost that only existed in Jacks' mind. He wrote magnificent tracks that appeared in newspapers and magazines, but never appeared in public.

Chablis interjected, "Yes, I remember his eloquence well, as I was still in university. He called them ramblings from the edge. The truth is that he also disappeared at almost the same time as Jack when he climbed Everest. Manley Martinez was an obnoxious firebrand in many ways, but a man of true intelligence."

They talked for sometime longer until Chablis remembered her appointment she had with Roy Blount, and tearing herself away from her kind friends sallied forth to her rendezvous. At the Manhattan Club, she was admitted with some reluctance, as they still were disgusted that members would actually invite a woman into the staid environs of the club, but the law of New

PURSUIT

York said they could no longer discriminate according to gender. So what choice did the club have? Roy was sitting in a leather lounger and bounded up to greet Chablis.

She had drinks with Roy, as there was no mention of the guest whom Chablis was to meet. Chablis expected the worst, but was cautious about asking just whom they were meeting. Roy very graciously suggested that the person he wanted her to meet preferred a more private place, so they should retire to his apartment in lower Manhattan and he would call ahead and tell his guest to meet them there. The plot was about to thicken.

PURSUIT

CHAPTER 3
MOST VALUABLE METAL

Upon arrival, there was no one waiting outside, so Roy suggested they go inside. The entrance to the parlour was accompanied with a brisk whisking off of Chablis' wrap by Roy as they walked toward the living room. He strolled over and turned on the gas fireplace and the gleam of the flames, the only light in the room, lit up a sparsely furnished room that bespoke of bachelorhood. Everything indicated the practical. The single window, Chablis noticed, was carefully curtained and barred, almost as if there was actually something worth hiding in the place. The place smelled of dust and mildew, as if it was not used very often. Suddenly, Chablis looked to her left where the dark was not penetrated by the fireplace light and by the arched doorway to the bedroom in an overstuffed chair sat a man of maybe 40, who was very distinguished looking. His face was most unprepossessing. There was a bull-dog's obstinacy and attachment about it.

Chablis, astute investigator, diagnosed at once that this was a man whose past was best unread, whose hand had in dark by-ways been persistently raised against his fellow man. It took no time at all to analyze his impression of Chablis as one of mild disdain as his gaze upon her never wavered. It was as if he was boring into her soul – driving himself into her mind to capture her thoughts.

J. Wayne Frye

PURSUIT

She was somewhat disgusted when Roy, almost whispering, said, "Meet my friend, Don Hart."

He got up, walked over and extended his hand to a somewhat shocked Chablis, who realized that the perpetrator of the bombing many years ago was indeed alive and well, having survived a dive off the GW. Cold as his death dealing grip was, she took the proffered hand cautiously. So this was the fanatic supposed to be long ago dead. She instantly felt as if she were in the presence of evil for some unknown reason.

Roy, a smirk on his face, said, "You should not be surprised Chablis. Hey, you know my penchant for the dramatic."

The meeting was what she should have expected she thought. Still, the coldness of the man was overwhelming. It was disconcerting for her to say the least. Anyway, this man had practiced what Chablis had often thought about. How many times had she contemplated just blowing up something out of hatred for the way things were?"

"Surprised," said Roy.

"I do confess some mild astonishment. It is seldom the sea, or in this case, the river, gives up its dead, and one does not meet anarchist celebrities like Mr. Hart every day."

PURSUIT

Hart laughed grimly. Chablis could see he was pleasantly tickled. Monstrous conceits sprout from the shedding of blood. He seemed to chuckle that he, outcast and rebel, was a celebrity. He could not resist self-aggrandizement. "I have been very active since the dive off the GW. Why even Carlos the Jackal did not wrought as much destruction as I have. Name almost any terrorist act of the past 10 years and I have probably had a hand in it. Why even Bin Laden consulted me at times. Of course, Cheney would probably have loved to consult with me, but I don't go in for individual torture. It is so unwieldy and unproductive. Still, he and his clown partner Bush did bring about much destruction. However, it was just a great recruitment tool for those of us so wrongly called terrorists. The real terrorists are those who sit in Congress and reside in the White House. They terrorize with impunity, but their day of reckoning is coming. Oh, it is coming."

Chablis detested the two men to which he referred. Bush and Cheney were arrogant, bombastic terrorists of the foulest kind. She even saw Hart as less of an evil, because he did not hide behind arrogant self-righteousness as those two did, and he was in the trenches, risking his life for what he believed in rather than sending out poor, patriotic brainwashed kids to die so he could puff out his chest and feel like a man. Bush and Cheney were cowards of the first order, but Hart, unlike them, was definitely no coward.

J. Wayne Frye

PURSUIT

"So, Swift is alive too," said Chablis.

Smiling, Hart replied, "Of course he is. He, too, has been very active the past 10 years. We have never been that far apart. We have been everywhere from Nepal to Nairobi. Ah, I am sure you remember the American soldiers who were slain there and that was attributed to Bin Laden. It was not Bin Laden. Believe me, he was not nearly the threat he was made out to be. He was just a good propaganda tool for the Americans."

"So, Roy, what is your purpose in bringing me into all this," said a perplexed Chablis.

"Well, I know you as a loyal and devoted believer in justice, even if it is justice for terrorists. These two brought disrepute to themselves by what they did in Manhattan, and they want to make recompense to the family of the vendor who was killed. I know you are a woman of integrity and can be trusted."

"Well, I don't make it a habit of helping murderers."

Hart took a deep breath and those intense eyes bore in on Chablis. "Look, we made a mistake. Sometimes innocents have to suffer so that many can be spared. Our aim is to always avoid civilian casualties, as we know that killing innocents is used by the USA as propaganda tool against those like us who just want justice in a world where there is none for anybody but the rich. We want to pay compensation and let the world know that our purpose is to defend people like her, not hurt them. I know what you think of me, but I also know you admire Che, and he used ruthless tactics when they were called for."

Chablis looked him directly in the eyes. "He used it on those who were themselves ruthless. He never brutalized the poor, the downtrodden, the marginalized."

Blount interrupted. "Look, we are not here to argue tactics. We just want to know will you find her family, find those who were affected by this mistake and see to it that they are compensated financially."

"And, of course, you want it publicized?"

Sighing, Blount replied, "Of course, what is wrong with that?"

"Nothing, I suppose," retorted Chablis. "Maybe we need to show the human face of terrorism."

Hart took a seat on the sofa beside Blount and said, "You see, we are about to triumph over evil. For at last, after long years of danger, delay, and disappointment, the dream of bringing down the empire of greed is at hand. You were once allied with a man calling himself *The Spirit of Che Guevara*, who disappeared into oblivion. He gave people hope, and things did change for awhile as the authorities feared him as they have feared no one before or after, but now he is forgotten, a footnote in history. We will make history!"

Chablis, beginning to feel the tedium of discourse with the two, said, "So, the struggle will finally end in triumph and capital will be tread underfoot; but before you do that you want to make things right in regards to one whom you feel has been wronged. There have been other innocents slaughtered. Why is this one being singled out for compensatory damages?"

Roy, seeming to hold something back, said, "She matters, as all the poor, as all those who struggle to keep their heads above water in this goddamn system of slavery matter. This was just one of many who mean nothing to the barons of greed. She is what we are fighting for."

Both the anarchists were sullen. Chablis, too, was serious in intent. She sensed there was something else that the two were not sharing, something that they were holding back which might be germane to what she was about to undertake. Yet, she felt sympathy for the relatives of the old woman killed inadvertently by anarchists who, and she almost laughed at this part, were just familiarizing themselves with their trade. Still, she was somewhat concerned that she might be abetting a plot to do mass harm, because the return of two anarchists did not portend good will obviously. There were sinister intentions, because they would not have resurfaced to do charitable work. It was not hyperbole to say that there was mischief afoot on a grand scale.

Chablis could not resist offering an observation. "You think that this act of atonement and some other terrorist manifestations will stir a sympathetic nerve worth noting and the very workers you think you are helping will somehow rise and crush their oppressors? I tell you such notions are fantastic in today's world where the poor and the middle class are too preoccupied with the mundane to entertain any hope against a maniacal moneyed class that has defeated them with assistance from a government that they have bought with their ill-gotten gains. How can a few scattered incendiaries or dynamiters, ceaselessly dodging the law, hope to defy a state that is devoted to the privileged class?"

Roy and Don stared at one another with a look of determination as Chablis continued. "The whole idea is ridiculous in today's world where the head of UNICEF, which is supposed to look after the poor children of the world, rides around in a chauffeured Rolls Royce and draws a salary of over one million dollars a year. In a world where almost every charity has million dollar a year executives we are supposed to believe people really care. Nobody cares anymore. If they did they would stop donating to these nefarious causes that play on people's compassion to put money in the pockets of hypocritical, greedy manipulative bastards. The public makes heroes out of royal whores like Diana who used photo ops to con the public into thinking she cared about the poor. It is all public relations today. Fool the public into thinking the rich and privileged give a damn. That old saying that people get the government they deserve rings true in a world where the poor vote against their own interests, because they are manipulated into believing less government is going to make their lives better, that capitalism is going to improve their lot, that somehow one party loves Jesus more than the other and that in the end the party that loves Jesus the most is going to help them rise like a phoenix from the ashes of despair to stroll through the streets of heaven that are paved with gold. The only gold these people will ever see is the gold adorning the arrogant assholes who have them all fooled into believing there is a hereafter filled with hope and promise."

Really on a roll now, Chablis took a deep breath as the two men sat mesmerized by her passion. "Until people stop believing in fairy tales and concentrate on the here and now, nothing will change. Muslin, Christian, Jew; it makes no difference what religion, none reach to the heart of what the problem is, religion itself, which has compromised humanity in search of that which does not exist. If people want heaven, they need to make it here on earth, because it is not going to be on the clouds in the sweet bye and bye. When you die, it is over. You two speak of struggle such as one man might wage against a mob in the street. It is not for this that Che died a martyr's death. It is not to be shot by soldiers or hunted by police that will bring people up from their knees."

Don reached in his pocket, and said as he did, "Do you wish to guess what weapon will be used to facilitate change? Take this piece of stuff in your hand, and tell me what you think of it," he said as he produced a small plate, apparently of silvery grey metal, of about ten square inches of surface, and one-tenth of an inch or so in thickness.

Chablis examined it carefully as Don said, "Now take careful note of its hardness and texture."

Chablis did so, and she noticed it was like absolutely no other metal she had ever felt before as it appeared weightless. There was also intense warmth to it.

"It is like no other metal I have ever felt. There seems to be no weight to it. It is almost as if it is a feather rather than metal. And the colour is not what one would expect of metal. It is, well, it is the colour of a cardboard box."

PURSUIT

Roy, a look of extreme smugness on his face, said, "It is extraordinary. Any idea what it can be used for?"

"No, can't say that I do."

Don leaned forward a bit, and said, "I found that in the old lady's food cart. After the explosion, I realized my mistake and tried to help the old lady, tried to see if she might have some life left in her. All she did was look downward at the mangled cart and seemingly, with her eyes, pointed at the bin beside of the hotdog steamer. I quickly opened it and this was in there. She said nothing. She just died. I took it, and ever since then I have tried to figure out its importance. It took ten years, but I finally did. It is a most extraordinary hunk of metal, and it comes from a place and time that makes it more powerful than anyone could ever imagine. You interested in its power?"

"I am."

"You will see its power eventually, Chablis. Meantime, please find the relatives of the unfortunate foot-cart lady. It is important to me, important to all who sincerely want justice for the downtrodden. If you require a retainer, we will be more than willing to pay whatever you want."

"I will let you know about a retainer, but maybe this one is on the house."

PURSUIT

The two men smiled at her, as both knew this would not be about money to her, but about justice.

Chablis was now less hesitant about getting involved, as holding that piece of metal had piqued her curiosity. Anyway, she was interested in exploring just what these two had in mind. If they were about to commit some atrocious atrocity, she felt that she might be more valuable on the inside than on the outside. She hated working with the authorities who represented the moneyed class, but she still felt a certain loyalty a nation that had opened up opportunity for a poor Mexican transsexual. Yet, she would only go so far in her loyalty.

Don Hart graciously excused himself, leaving Roy and Chablis alone. Chablis sensed that Roy was not sure of her intentions as he was always fearful of a spy from the police or government authorities infiltrating his extremely private domain devoted to socialist causes. They talked until about 1:00 AM. When she rose to go, Roy grabbed her and pulled her close. He whispered to her. "I have always found you sexually exciting Chablis. Let me taste the forbidden fruit? How about it?"

Chablis, never above using her feminine charms to get information, saw an opening. She said, "Come on, Roy, it is no use playing the mystery

J. Wayne Frye

man any longer. I shall know everything eventually. Trust me with what you know about what is going to happen." She then went limp in his arms and allowed him a slow, lingering, passionate kiss.

Roy backed off, smiled at her and walked over to a bookshelf. He took down a ring binder like ones used by school kids, opened it very purposefully, as if he knew the exact page he wanted. He began to read:

"Man faces great impediments to enlightenment. Navigating the air was man's greatest dream, and it came to fruition because two intrepid dreamers refused to let the sceptics plant the seeds of doubt in their minds. There are elements in the world of which no one knows. One such element is the metal tellurium, which is so light a ship built of it that is the size of a football field will weigh only a few kilos. It is indestructible and it is available in only one place in the entire world, and I and only one other know its location. When science shall have discovered some moving power greatly lighter than any we yet know, in all probability the problem will be used for ill rather than good. Alas, I will not record my secret here for fear it might fall into the wrong hands."

Roy put the notebook back in the shelf and said, "We are on the cusp of a game-changer Chablis. Believe me. I have waited all my life for the opportunity to make the world into the utopia it should be if only the greedy bastards could be brought to heel.'

He pointed toward the notebook he had put back on the shelf. "That man is long dead, but he wrote of what he saw as a boon to all mankind, but he feared that it would fall into the wrong hands, just as the atomic bomb fell into the wrong hands. Could you imagine the good that atomic power could have been used for had the American warmongers not been the ones who controlled all that power? Just imagine how much better off the world would be today had that power fallen into more capable hands. Why was that power used to kill innocent men, women and children? It could have been such a magnificent boon to the world, a chance to lift everyone out of poverty could have been realized, but the Americans saw only its power as a military weapon to bring nations to their knees and promulgate the society of greed all over the world, making all bow before the greed that is like an infectious disease destroying everything in its sight. Oh, you felt power tonight girl, power that can be used to destroy those who would bring humanity into the gutter of greed. That power is in the possession of those who want to use it to benefit mankind, not harm him."

Chablis knew instantly that the metal she had held in her hands was tellurium. The old woman who was killed that day somehow had gotten hold of what was probably the most valuable piece of metal in the world.

CHAPTER 4
A WHIRLPOOL OF MISCHIEF

Chablis was a woman who loved romance, and the fact that she had left Roy without a sexual dalliance was actually troubling her, as she had always wondered what it would be like to have a sexual encounter with him. When she awakened the next morning, with that preying on her mind, she felt an instant rise between her legs as she imagined what it would be like to have Roy's tongue buried deep into her anal cavity that was a delight to all men who were lucky enough to enjoy a dalliance with her. Some would shy away from it, but she was always meticulously clean and prepared for action. She had an opening that was probably wider than most women's vaginas as she had trained herself for love making from the rear like it was an art form. She got a little tingle in her sphincter as she remembered how as an adolescent she had used a homemade butt-plug that she wore all day to prepare herself for the deflowering that came about one day in the factory office where the man she wanted most in her village bent her over a desk and made her a woman. She reached down and began to pull back and forth on her member, moaning with delight as she recalled the loveliness of the day she was deflowered. She reached a crescendo with her furious pounding up and down; up and down until she squirted her liquid love juice all over here naked stomach, letting out a sigh of relief.

J. Wayne Frye   77

PURSUIT

Feeling exhilarated, she came down to breakfast, picked up the phone and called Aaron Adams to review the previous night's situation. They were both almost on the verge of laughter at the faith in what seemed the wild vagaries of the two men. The discussion of the weird aspects of the evening had lost some of its vividness and given place to a suspicion that what occurred was almost dreamlike. Then, she went back to the little piece of metal she held in her hand and wondered aloud why it was so important. Aaron very quickly told her, "be careful. That object is priceless."

She said, "Aaron, if anything worth the mentioning is to be known, if I stay in touch with them a great deal will be revealed."

Aaron was getting worried, "Chablis, I will tail you. I don't trust these guys, and I also don't trust the authorities, so I say we hold off on going to them. You and I both know that the government practices its own form of anarchy, except theirs is legitimized, which often makes it an even more sinister form of anarchy."

"Aaron, I just thought of something. You know Robert Hernandez is executor of Donald Perez's estate."

"Right."

"I just thought of something strange."

PURSUIT

Aaron replied, "OK, Let's hear it."

"Well, last night I did not think of it, but I noticed a name on the front of that notebook that Roy read from. Just a last name was all."

Astute detective that he was, Aaron interjected, "Perez?"

"Damn, you must be a detective."

"Yeah, a damn good one, too. Could be coincidence, but it is worth a look. So, you want me to do the leg work on finding the food cart vendor's name and relatives?"

"Actually, I know you have the Murphy case to finish up Aaron. Lynton is in town with Channa and Ingrid. I will let her do it. You know how she loves to play detective."

"Yeah, good idea. Speaking of playing, that is one woman I would like to play with."

"Keep your pants zipped. She is spoken for, and, unlike me, she is not promiscuous."

Chablis called Lynton and gave her the details on the food cart murder. Lynton, thrilled at the chance to be a detective, said she would get right on it. Afterwards, Chablis got a call from Lena and passed the morning with small talk.

PURSUIT

Lena invited her to Sunday tea and Chablis willingly accepted. She found herself wondering what sex would be like with another woman. Was she beginning to find Lena sexually arousing? She shivered a bit and told herself, "no, no, can't do it."

First stop for Chablis was the home of Robert Perez. She had not seen him for some time, but was anxious to find out more about the inheritance, but wanted to be certain not to seem overly eager. She wondered if she should bring up the notebook with the name Perez on it. No, it was just a coincidence she thought, nothing would come of it, so why bother?

It was late afternoon when Chablis reached Perez's estate on Long Island. The maid who admitted her said he was not at home, as he had an important meeting that came up on the spur of the moment, but that he would be home shortly.

Chablis was ushered into the library and told to make herself comfortable. She took a seat in one of the exquisite walnut chairs with thick cushions on it. The bay window which lit the library looked out onto a well-manicured lawn that was so green it appeared as if someone had just painted it with semi-gloss. There was little within the library to catch the eye. She got up and walked around. Exploring the walls she came across a shelf full of musky books.

PURSUIT

The books primarily dealt with mathematics and engineering, along with a variety of treatises on political economy and the sciences, evidently mementos of the son who had perished on Everest, where his body, no doubt, lay permanently covered by ice and snow which would preserve it until the global warming reached levels above 25,000 feet. Of course, the Republicans would continue to deny global warming until their asses were singed with pitchforks from hell, which is where most of them belonged.

While glancing through some the books and noting the numerous traces of careful study, the thought struck Chablis that there were never any photographs of Perez's son. She had been there many times, but had never been favoured with opportunity to see what he looked like. Was it because memories of him were too painful? Yet, he did have photographs of his wife around. Being left with nothing to do, she noticed some old photo albums lying on the desk in the corner. Why not take a gander she thought.

Loosening the clasp of one that lay near, she flipped through it nonchalantly. She was not really all that interested in the photos, but then she asked herself why she was doing this? What was the driving force behind the search? What did she suspect? True, there were mediocre denizens in plenty, shoals of cousins, sisters, and aunts, hordes of nonentities.

J. Wayne Frye 81

PURSUIT

As she got toward the end of the album, there was one loose photo on the next to the last page. She turned it over on the back and it was marked in red ink – Jack at age 29. That would make him 39 now, if he were alive, thought Chablis.

It was the face of a young man evidently of high capacity and unflinching resolution. A slight moustache brushed the upper lip, and set off a clear-cut but somewhat cunning mouth. There was a sublime tinge of confidence in his bearing that indicated a somewhat determined young man with certain contemptuousness for authority. Yes, it was there, definitely a man who could easily defy authority.

Chablis was contemplating with much vigour as she stared at the photo when she heard the front door of the house open. There was no bell, so it must be Mr. Hernandez returning she thought.

He strolled in, greeted her with a pleasant smile which showed up in curious contrast to the look of depression so familiar to Chablis, as he had mourned his son for years and then his wife of late. Yet, the obvious buoyancy of his spirit seemed so uncharacteristic of the man Chablis had known for some time. Chablis had seen a man who had been raised from the dead when she was at Roy's house, and she wondered if maybe Hernandez had heard news that his son had been found alive after all this time, as he was so happy that it was like a miracle. He moved toward her with vigour and had his hand out. "Chablis my dear, it is so nice to see you. My, how beautiful you look. Then again, you are always beautiful."

His was an expressive face, and the shadows upon it were few enough to warrant that inference. Probably he had smoothed over the past and finally found meaning to his life after all this time. The death of his wife was not nearly as hard on him as the continuing saga of a son who had been lost on a climb up Mt. Everest, the mountain that had brought death to so many. The boy was an only child, and there was now no one to pass the family mantle onto. With Robert, it was the end of the line of the Hernandez family, which had originally migrated with the Spanish conquerors to the Philippines where all but two had been wiped out in a small-pox epidemic. Those two had migrated to the USA, but on the way one died of severe dysentery on the ship. Robert had survived and become rich, but the riches meant nothing to him without his son.

"Well, Chablis, it is pleasant to see you. As you know, when things are settled you have a tidy sum coming to you from a man who greatly admired you. Donald never tired of talking about what a fine woman you are. I heard you were going on vacation."

"I was, but some things came up."

PURSUIT

"Ah, the detecting business is always full of surprises. I hear that famous demonologist, Lynton Viñas, is in town. I hope I shall see that cute little dynamic dynamo as she is called by Wayne in his books."

"I am sure you will. She is helping me out on a case as we speak and is in a will I here."

The conversation wandered for some time among various topics, when Chablis casually mentioned that she had been looking over the photo album.

"Kind of boring looking at old black and white photos, especially mine as most of the people I know are dead. When you reach my age, there are few people you have a history with left around."

"Oh, I found it interesting." As she finished, Chablis reached down and picked up the photo of his son and handed it to him. The effect was noticeable. Obviously, he had forgotten it was in the album.

"Have you never seen that face before? It is that of Jack, my misguided son, of whom you must have heard from time to time probably; although people tend to never mention him because of the pain it causes me. Poor boy! Ten years have rolled by since his death. It has been ten gruelling years of intense misery."

PURSUIT

He was admirably cool about his son, but Chablis sensed there was something he was not sharing. Hey, she was a detective and detectives are like psychologists, they can read people's body language.

That is when Chablis decided to drop the bombshell, because she had recognized Jack Hernandez. He was 10 years older with nice grey hair that made him distinguished looking, a few kilos heavier and actually better looking. Still there was no mistaking the fact that Jack Hernandez and Don Hart were one and the same. So, Jack had never disappeared on the trek up Everest. It was just a ploy to keep people from connecting Hart to Hernandez. The truth was pure and simple – Jack Hernandez was the terrorist, and Don Hart, and Chablis had been in the same room with him at Roy Blount's apartment."

"My dear Mr. Hernandez, Jack is alive and you know it. Two days ago I was with him."

Hernandez's face turned white and betrayed complete discomfiture mingled with obvious signs of alarm. He made no attempt to contradict Chablis.

Stunned, he eased down into a nearby chair. "What will you do?" he stammered with deep trepidation. "Are you also in on the secret? Are you going to the authorities?"

J. Wayne Frye

PURSUIT

"Of course not. At least not yet. I just met him a couple of days ago. Roy Blount trusts me, and I will try my best not to betray that trust. You can trust me too. I know he is the anarchist responsible for that abominable mishap ten years ago. He is your son, and I understand your devotion. That is enough for me. You can be assured of my silence unless something unusual comes into play."

His distress was visibly abated. "Thanks Chablis. I feel I can rely on you to lend a helping hand if I need it. I know you might not believe it, but he is a changed man. If I can get him back overseas, away from this country that is filled with hate rather than compassion, maybe he can salvage his life. Maybe it is not too late. I am living on the edge, fearing for his safety."

"I can happily reassure you that he is indeed safe, as safe as a fugitive can be, and I think he is in good hands with Roy."

Sighing, Hernandez said, "I am not sure of Roy Blount. He does watch over him I know, as he sees him as a grand defender of socialism, but I fear he is also a tutor in vice. I think it was he who led him astray originally, and even introduced him to Manly Martinez and Bob Swift. And what is he now but an outlaw in the shadow of the executioner, in a country that loves retribution. I am so afraid for him Chablis. He may have done wrong, but he is all I have left in the world."

PURSUIT

He started weeping and Chablis moved to him, and standing by the chair, put her right arm around his shoulder, patting it. She waited patiently until the tempest of emotion subsided and in a soothing voice said, "It will be O.K. Don't worry. Chablis Louise Chavez is on the case."

One need not be too scrupulous when sufferers such as this plead for compassion. Chablis knew that no good was likely to come of his son, but she could not burden him with the truth of the situation. His son had courted disaster before, and from what Chablis had seen, he was now ready to commit a supreme act of folly that would likely lead to his incarceration or death.

"You knew of his dual life as Don Hart and Jack Hernandez, then?" said Chablis.

"I did. It was I who suggested after he escaped from the Hudson River dive that he was not identifiable as Don Hart since no photos existed of the man called Hart. He decided to leave on an expedition to climb Everest, and while there, he managed to disappear and his fellow climbers assumed he was dead, as did I until a few days ago. He said he never told me to spare me the shame he had brought to me. He decided to return apparently at the urging of his lover Manly Martinez who seemed to think they would no longer be recognized after some plastic surgery and ten long years. Of course, Swift is also back."

PURSUIT

"He has told you nothing of his plans while here?"

"No, he just let me know he was alive to ease my pain. He says that he will see me at the right time in the right place, and that it is better we not see each other right now for fear of discovery. He says he shall be here only a short while and then it is off to the Middle East where it is safer. Well, safer as long as the USA doesn't decide to obliterate another country to bring it democracy that is."

Chablis knew that Jack was deceiving him. There would be no meeting as it was just too unsafe. Hell, the Feds probably had the house under surveillance for years just in case. Time and money made no difference to the U.S. government. It never forgot and never forgave. Yet, she saw no need to destroy the illusions that had brought him a bit of happiness. Let him believe in a reformed son and his prospects for a normal life. Were he to suspect that mischief was again being plotted by his son, what a cruel scattering of his hopes would follow. And maybe, just maybe Chablis could convince them of the follies involved in trying to change things in a god-forsaken country where change was a dirty word, almost as dirty as socialism.

Meanwhile, Chablis had become aware that nothing of importance to her quest was to be

PURSUIT

drawn from dear Mr. Hernandez. So, she rose to leave, not, however, without having promised that, should his son again run across her path, she would stand by him for Mr. Hernandez's sake in a possible hour of danger.

He profusely thanked Chablis, because he knew her to be a woman of her word. It meant so much to him to know that she was on his side, and he said that he would be settling Donald's estate soon and get her the money she was left.

Chablis told him not to worry that the money was not important. What was really important was that he take care of himself and not worry too much about his son, as things would work out alright in the end. Of course, she sensed that things would not work out fine. There had been a look in Jack's eyes that portended an ill omen in his future. There was a fatalistic gleam in his eyes that indicated he was ready to face doom in order to fulfill what he obviously felt was his destiny.

As she made her way to the door, Hernandez took her arm and affectionately held onto it as if she offered solace from the storms of despair that had surrounded him for so long. Of course, she knew that she could offer little comfort other than words. It was as if she knew the die had been cast and the colour was blood red. The blood of Jack and how many others she wondered. Things were not looking good at all.

PURSUIT

Yes thought Chablis, as she walked out the door and looked up at a greying sky. She was right in the middle of a whirlpool of mischief.

\

PURSUIT

CHAPTER 5
IT IS THE WAY WE ARE PROGRAMMED

While Chablis was visiting with Mr. Hernandez, Lynton was busy tracking down the family of Henrietta Hobson, the lady with the food cart who was in the wrong place at the wrong time. Chablis had informed Lynton of the strange metal that she was privy to examining at Roy Blount's apartment. Of course, she also let her know that the metal had come from Henrietta Hudson's food cart, taken by the terrorist responsible for her death, Don Hart, or Jack Hernandez if preferred.

That morning, Lynton sent Channa and Ingrid to do research on the attack itself at the library. It had been ten years and when Lynton knocked on Pamela Hobson's door, the woman of maybe 50 with two front teeth missing and a dour look on her face, stood in disbelief that someone was interested in the story of her mom's death after all those years. After all, her mother was poor, and the poor are quickly forgotten as, somehow, they just are not that important in a society where everyone is judged by the size of their bank account rather than the size of their character.

She invited Lynton in and apologized for the disarray of her home that was more like a pig sty than a house. There was very little furniture, and when Lynton took a seat on the sofa, she felt the springs give way.

J. Wayne Frye   91

PURSUIT

Pamela said, "My mom was a fine woman who cared about her children very deeply. Our father left us when we were small, and she tried very hard to give us a good home, but she had no education, no connections and very little hope. She worked three jobs for years, and finally saved enough money to get her own food cart. She did pretty well, too, and was very proud of herself. Hey, my sister and I were proud of her, too."

Lynton, sympathetic with the plight of all who are, by circumstance of birth, relegated to a life of poverty, said, "Well, I am sure she was a fine woman, and I represent a party who wants to help out her family."

"Help out? What you mean help?"

"Financial compensation to help with the loss of your mother."

"You got to be kidding. Why would the government want to do something after all these years? Hey, if she had been somebody important, the government would have helped immediately. Remember the 9/11 victims? The stockbrokers, the lawyers, the ones with good jobs, their families got more than the families of janitors and the uneducated. Just a way for the government to tell you some people are more important than others. Try telling the janitor's family that he isn't as important as a stockbroker."

PURSUIT

Fully sympathetic, Lynton replied, "I know what you mean. We live in a world where those at the top are catered to while those at the bottom simply don't matter. However, is not the government that wants to compensate you. It is an anonymous source who would like to give you and your sister some financial compensation for your loss."

"I don't understand. Who would want to do that?"

"I am not at liberty to say Ms. Hudson. I am sorry about that."

"You know," replied Pamela Hudson in a contemplative manner, "my mom said she was set for life and that we would be too. She said she had something that would be worth millions, something that she got from a bum in the Bowery, gave it to her because she was always giving him free hotdogs. Told her to guard it with her life and one day talk to the government, the CIA or the NSA about it and they would reward her big time. Anyway, we looked for it years and years after her death, but never found anything."

Lynton, curious about the bum, said, "This man who gave it to her. Did you ever hear his name?"

"Name, name? Well, I can't recall. No, don't think so. Just a minute. Let me get my sister, maybe she knows."

PURSUIT

She turned her head toward the hallway and shouted, "Sherry, get in here a minute."

In America, the rich get the best of everything, but the poor are not entitled to medical care, dental care, decent shelter or a living wage. In Sherry, you could see a woman who had been beaten down by poverty. In fact, poverty is generational, almost hereditary. If your parents are poor the chances are you will be poor, too. Sherry hobbled in on legs that had huge lesions on them, making it rather painfully to a chair across from Lynton. She eased into it and said, "Howdy ma'am. So what can I do for you?"

Lynton went through the same story she had told Pamela and then asked if she knew the name of the man who gave her mother the item that would make her rich.

"Sure, but my sister and I just laughed mostly. I mean who is going to make us rich. Like some bum gives my mom something to make us rich. Why would he do that? Why wouldn't he make himself rich? Why give it to my mom? Hey, this is America; you get rich here if your parents are rich. Land of opportunity, bull-shit, land of nepotism where the rich get richer and the poor get poorer. His name I remember, because it was funny, real funny. A name like that you never forget. Nesmond Nimrod was it. Now how is that for a name, Nesmond Nimrod?"

Pamela interjected, "Yeah, now I remember. Been so long I just forgot. So yeah, Nesmond Nimrod was it. So, anyway sis, this young woman says we are getting some compensation from somebody unnamed for mom's death. How about that?"

"Bull-shit! That will be the day when someone gives us something."

Lynton got up and said as she prepared to leave, "It is coming soon. That is all I can say."

Sherry, still sceptical, said, "Sure, I'll believe it when I see it."

As Chablis stood at the door, she seemed hesitant to leave. Pamela said, "Go ahead; you still want to ask something. Go ahead, ask."

"Did this Nimrod ever have a romantic interest in your mom?"

Henrietta replied, with a shrug of the shoulders and a smile, "My mom wasn't bad looking in her day. I think she was interested, but figured someone on Skid Row was a poor prospect. She did say once that she thought he was in love with her."

"Do you know if he is still alive Pamela? I would like to talk to him."

PURSUIT

"Alive? I am not sure." She turned and hollered back to her sister. "Sherry, any idea if Nesmond Nimrod is still alive?"

"Sure, as far as I know, he is still on Skid Row. Just go down to the Bowery. With a name like that, he won't be hard to find."

Lynton excused herself and headed for Skid Row after phoning Chablis, who told her to go to the Bowery Bonaventure Hotel on Broadway. Only in America, Lynton thought, would one of the worst poverty laden areas be a tourist attraction. Ever since the 1950's, tour buses had plied through the area pointing it out as a place where those whose luck had run out resided in misery and despair. The rich and famous often wound up there when drugs, alcohol or a run of business reverses destroyed their exalted place in the society of greed. It was the place where dreams came to die.

Lynton had lived in abject poverty as a child, but as she walked the debris-filled streets of the Bowery, she felt the real pangs of poverty in a society that was capable of so much more. In the Philippines, poverty was mildly excusable, but in the USA with all its wealth, there simply was no excuse. The Bowery was the place where one realized the folly of an economic system with no heart, no core to its soul, no blood of compassion coursing through its veins, no air of fairness in its lungs, no legs of hope upon which to stand. This was the body of America – the real body of a nation that had long ago lost its way. The climb up for most people was just simply too steep.

Chablis was standing in the hotel lobby waiting as Lynton walked in. Chablis and Aaron had worked a case recently that involved locating a man who had disappeared into the bowels of the Bowery to avoid his family and having to watch them live in poverty because of a business reversal. They were an example of what real love was all about, because all they wanted to do was take care of their loved one, look after him as he had looked after them for so many years and let him know that the money, the luxurious home, the fancy cars were not as important as his love. His two sons who had been part of his empire had taken menial jobs after the bankruptcy, his wife had gone back to work as a waitress and his daughter got a job as a secretary at a plumbing company. These were people who valued what really counted and did not base their love on what someone could give them. In the end, she and Aaron actually felt they had failed, because the man simply could not face his family and what he perceived as his failure. He hanged himself in a dark alleyway, leaving a note of apology for being unable to face life without his riches. In the end, the material things had meant more than the love of his family. Unfortunately, that was the norm, not the exception in a society that judges everything in dollars and cents. Welcome to capitalism.

Walking into the Bowery Bonaventure Hotel for Lynton was like a stroll into a valley of despair. Sitting around in the dingy lobby, which had once harboured wealthy patrons were the dregs of a society based on greed whose wealth had been a transitory illusion that they believed would never end. True, some had never possessed wealth, but some had tasted the fruits of capitalism at its height, only to find out that they had built their empires on shifting sand.

Chablis greeted Lynton with a hug, and in this den of despair these two magnificently, gorgeously captivating creatures of beauty shone their light of grandeur in a lobby of lost hope. It was as if scintillating sunshine had bathed a dark hole of hopelessness with a ray of radiance that lifted the spirits of lost souls toward heaven where two angels of light were ready to wrap their compassionate arms around you and let you feel the warmth of their love.

The unkempt, shabbily-dressed desperate men, lounging in dour despondency on dirty old chairs and sofas, looked longingly up at these two and felt an immediate buoyancy of benevolence as the women smiled at them, showing not distasteful disdain and reviling disgust, but respect and compassion.

PURSUIT

Chablis whispered to Lynton, "Don't be afraid. These men are actually kinder, gentler and more respectful than most men you would find on Wall Street or in the office towers of Manhattan."

Lynton replied, "I am more afraid of the wealthy than the poor. The rich are always suspect, because they never have enough. On the other hand, the poor can usually be relied on to lend a helping hand. They have compassion, while the rich only have greed."

Chablis motioned for Lynton to follow her to the desk clerk, who was a man of maybe 60 but looked 75 or 80. He had missing teeth, as most elderly poor do, since dental care was a privilege afforded only those two could afford it. The poor were not entitled to keep their teeth.

The clerk, remembering Chablis from the earlier case, when she had been looking for the man who hanged himself, said, "Damn if it isn't Chablis Louise Chavez. How you doing girl?"

"Fine thanks," she said as she pointed to Lynton and continued, "This is my friend Lynton. She would like to ask you some questions. O.K.?"

"Sure, glad to help anyway I can, Chablis."

Lynton, smiling cordially, said, "I am looking for a man named Nesmond Nimrod. "

PURSUIT

Seeming to think for awhile without a response, after a few seconds he responded. "Nimrod, Nimrod. Nimrod, Nimrod. You know I heard that name before. He then shouted out to those sitting in the lobby, who were all staring at Chablis and Lynton, "Any of you guys know a Nesmond Nimrod?"

They all shook their heads except one man who was sitting by the lobby window. He rose, walked over toward them and stopped right by the desk where he leaned on the counter. "I know Nesmond, but he ain't the friendly type. Prefers to keep to himself. Seems he is leery of people, especially people who look like cops, and you two women do."

Lynton was surprised that he would say that about her, as she had never been particularly fond of cops, as they too often oppressed the poor rather than helped, and Chablis had far too frequently been at the receiving end of racial profiling as her Hispanic heritage and allure made cops think she was selling sex. She reached into her purse and brought out her private investigator ID, flashed it in front of him and said, "Private heat, and she is my friend, Lynton. We are simply trying to find out some information on someone who is due some cash. I know what you mean about cops. I come from a place where they aren't your friends, but rather your enemies. So, believe me, I have no interest in hassling Mr. Nimrod."

PURSUIT

"O.K., I'm Art Carson, come with me and I will take you to where he usually hangs out. You will need me there to make sure he understands you aren't the heat and don't bring trouble."

Chablis nodded in the affirmative and signalled for Lynton to follow her. The man seemed pleased to have two gorgeous women in tow as he sashayed down the debris littered back street that was filled with people in doorways and lying prone on the hard concrete. This was the real face of American capitalism that was hidden from view. European capitalism, Canadian capitalism and Australian capitalism had a somewhat more human face as the rich were not pandered to as blatantly as they were in the USA. American capitalism was an abomination, a blight on society that was the result of the rich being exalted and pampered while the poor were castigated and criticized for being poor. How ironic that the poor were the ones admonished when the real culprits were those at the top who felt they should not be required to pay their fair share. Fairness and capitalism were alien terms in the United States of America.

The stench of human excrement and urine hung over the alleyway like a cloud of hopelessness. These were people reduced to the basest existence because of an economic system that relegated a permanent underclass to misery so that a few could live lives of splendorous excess. Oddly, this abomination was only a short walk from Wall Street where the cause of all this misery was ballyhooed and exalted as the hope of mankind.

Art Carson, very slowly made his way through the dank alleyway with the girls right behind. He looked over his shoulder, shook his head and sighed. Ain't used to seeing so much misery, uh? Welcome to our world ladies. It ain't pretty, but it is the real America. The one nobody wants to admit exists."

Chablis, ever the astute observer of the human condition, said, "Oh, I am familiar with it Art. It is what complacency gets you. People accept their lot. What all of you should do is band together and march on the mayor's office, walk down Park Avenue and show the world what unfettered capitalism does to people. However, you will not do it, because you have all been conditioned to accept your fate as your own fault, not the fault of the system."

"You pretty smart lady. That is right. We just roll over and say kick me again. Me, I used to be a plumbing contractor. Had it all, Mercedes, fancy home on Long Island, but thanks to Mr. Bush, I lost it all when he crashed the economy. Of course, he is still living high on the hog. Got himself a nice pension from the taxpayers that he doesn't even need, while we people are told that we are the drain on the system. I say bull-shit."

PURSUIT

Just as he finished, there, in a far corner, lay a man with bushy white hair of maybe 60, curled up in a fetal position. Art walked up and bent down over him. "Nesmond, it is Art. How you doing buddy?"

"Art, howdy there. I'm OK. How about you?"

"Fine, fine Nesmond, but I got two very attractive ladies here want to talk to you. What ya' say? They ain't cops."

Getting slowly into a sitting position, looking up at Chablis and Lynton, he smiled slightly and nodded his head yes. The two women moved closer and said "hello."

"Hi ladies. Pardon my appearance. I am not used to meeting classy ladies down here."

Chablis said, "Well, speaking for myself, I am not that classy. Now maybe my friend here is, but I am just a down and out private eye looking for some answers. I think you might have a few."

"Lady, I used to make a living giving people answers to complex problems, until I became a liability to the government. Now, I don't make much of an effort to give anybody any answers, but for a good-looking duo like you two, I might make an exception. Just what can old Nesmond Nimrod do for you?"

PURSUIT

Lynton, who had been with the Hobson sisters, chimed in, "You remember a lady named Henrietta Hobson?"

"Damn right I do. Nicest lady I ever met. She used to push her cart on the downtown section of Park. You know the area where it goes from high price, to moderate price and then to low price. No business for her uptown, people think they are too high class to eat food from a cart, but she'd push it down to the lower part and make a few bucks. I used to work a squeegee there, cleaning the windshields of the high and mighty. Never got much, though. They just waved me off with a sneer. Anyway, she'd give me a free hotdog and a coke almost every day. Gave freebies to some others like me, too. That lady had a good heart."

"Lynton continued, "So, one day you repaid her by giving her something."

"I did do that. So, you are trying to find out about the metal?"

Chablis piped in, "That and a few other things."

He looked around the alley, almost as if he suspected there was some sinister person lurking around, listening to the conversation, but there was no one within earshot. Still, he seemed overly cautious as he bent over slightly and whispered, "Too many prying eyes around here."

PURSUIT

Chablis, looking back toward the alley entrance, said, "So, we can go to a café and get a booth. Would that make you feel better?"

Smiling, he said, "If you buy me lunch."

Letting out a light laugh, Chablis looked over at Carson and said, "OK, I will buy you both lunch."

"Nope," replied a very determined Nimrod, you ladies are on business, but my friend Art here ain't involved, and the less he knows the safer he is. Don't want him to get himself in any trouble."

Chablis reached in her purse and took out a 20 dollar bill, handed it to Art and said, "Thanks for your help."

Art, without hesitation, started to walk away as he looked back over his shoulder and said, "Real pleasure ladies, a real pleasure."

While all this was going on, Ingrid and Channa were busy in the Manhattan public library reviewing documents in regards to the almost comic attempt on the life of the royal leech, the Prince of Wales. It appeared that he had been busy waving to the adoring royal worshipers, who somehow found comfort in their mundane lives by bowing and scrapping in the presence of someone who had never done anything worthwhile in his entire life, and in the process never saw anything.

J. Wayne Frye   105

PURSUIT

When they heard an explosion nearby, the taxpayer supplied police escort immediately whisked him away, for royal personages were so valuable to mankind they had to be protected at all costs. Then, something caught Channa's eye on the microfiche screen. At the bottom of the article, a small photograph appeared showing the food cart in little pieces and the old lady lying in a pool of blood, but standing over to one side, seeming to try and avoid the camera by turning her head was someone that Channa recognized. It was none other than a very young-looking Lena Langley.

Channa and Ingrid looked at one another astonished by what they had found. What was Lena doing there that day? Channa, picking up her phone, immediately dialled Lynton's number. However, Lynton had turned off her phone to make certain that no one disturbed her and Chablis' talk with Nesmond Nimrod.

As Chablis and Lynton sat at the booth, watching Nesmond frantically devour his meal like it was going to be his last one, they tried to avoid disturbing him as he seemed to be enjoying it so much. It was Nimrod who broke the silence. "So, you ladies want to know about the metal. OK, but I warn you that knowing about it is dangerous."

Lynton looked at Chablis and laughingly said, "We live lives of danger and love it."

PURSUIT

Nimrod, very serious, said, "This is not a joking matter. I worked for the CIA Technological Intelligence Department. It actually, if you ask, does not exist. However, it does exist, believe me. It was our job to technologically improve intelligence gathering. Now, in the process, we turned up a metal that had been aboard the HMS Bounty, seems the mutineers took the metal with them when they wound up on Pitcairn Island."

Chablis interrupted, "Wait a minute. I remember an old movie about the Bounty. You talking about a ship from the 1700's right?"

"I am. Excuse me, you ladies are probably too young and too unschooled in history, no offence, but that is the way it is in the world today, history is what happened yesterday, not what happened 200 years ago. History for you people is what did the Kardashian whores do last night or what is Brittany Spears' latest hit. Let me give you a little ancient history." Thus, began Nesmond Nimrod's history lesson about the Bounty in earnest, as he began a most exciting tale.

"HMS Bounty was a small merchant vessel purchased by the Royal Navy for a botanical mission. The ship, under the command of William Bligh, was sent to the Pacific Ocean to acquire breadfruit plants and transport them to British possessions in the Indies. That mission was never completed due to a mutiny led by the acting

J. Wayne Frye 107

Master, Fletcher Christian. This was the famous Mutiny on the Bounty."

"The ship had been purchased by the Royal Navy for a single mission in support of an experiment: The acquisition of breadfruit plants from Tahiti, and the transportation of those plants to the Indies in the hope that they would grow well there and become a cheap source of food for slaves."

Finally, Nimrod put down his fork, leaned back and relaxed after a hearty meal. He continued. "In June 1787, William Bligh was appointed Captain of Bounty. In December 1787, Bounty sailed for Tahiti. For a full month, the crew attempted to take the ship around Cape Horn, but adverse weather prevented this. Bligh then proceeded east, rounding the southern tip of Africa and crossing the width of the Indian Ocean. However, on its way around the Horn of Africa, they passed what in modern day interpretations would be a ghost ship near what is today, Cape Town, South Africa."

"There is no record of any crew member from the Bounty boarding the ghost ship, and no record was ever made of the encounter in the Bounty's log. The captain did not want it known that he had not stopped to assist what could have been a sick crew. Bligh had one goal and that was getting to Tahiti. However, there was a dinghy, a small boat, tied to the stern of the ship and it was just bobbing up and down in the sea. According to one crew member there was a strange object in the bottom of the dinghy that was glistening brightly in the sun and giving off a low humming sound. They cut the boat's ropes and hoisted it onto the deck of the Bounty. There was a small piece of metal causing the hum, and Bligh took it to his cabin where it was kept until the Bounty reached Tahiti after 10 months at sea. It appears that Bligh began to change once that piece of metal was put in his cabin, and he could be heard talking to someone in his cabin; although no one but he was in there."

"Bligh and his crew spent five months in Tahiti, collecting and preparing over 1000 breadfruit plants to be transported. Bligh allowed the crew to live ashore and care for the potted breadfruit plants, and they became socialized to the customs and culture of the Tahitians. Many of the seamen had themselves tattooed in native fashion. Master's Mate Fletcher Christian married Maimiti, a Tahitian woman. Other of Bounty's seamen were also said to have formed "connections" with native women."

"After five months in Tahiti, Bounty set sail with her breadfruit cargo in 1789. Some 2000 kilometres west of Tahiti, near Tonga, mutiny broke out. Despite strong words and threats heard on both sides, the ship was taken bloodlessly and apparently without struggle by any of the loyalists except Bligh himself. Of the 42 men on board, 22 joined Christian in mutiny, two were passive, and 18 remained loyal to Bligh."

Chablis and Lynton were actually enjoying the exciting tale of the Bounty, moving to the edge of their seats, waiting for the next part. Nimrod continued. "The mutineers ordered Bligh and those loyal to him put adrift in a boat. Bligh sailed over 7000 kilometres and landed in Indonesia. Today, it is considered one of history's greatest sailing feats."

"The mutineers sailed for the island of Tubuai, where they tried to settle. After three months of bloody conflict with the natives, however, they went back to Tahiti. Sixteen of the mutineers, including the four loyalists, who had been unable to accompany Bligh, remained there. Immediately after setting the sixteen men ashore in Tahiti in September 1789, Fletcher Christian, eight other crewmen, six Tahitian men, and 11 women set sail in Bounty hoping to elude the Royal Navy. According to a journal kept by one of Christian's followers, the Tahitians were actually kidnapped when Christian set sail without alerting them, the purpose of this being to acquire the women. The mutineers passed through the Fiji and Cook Islands, but feared that they would be found there. Continuing their quest for a safe haven, in January 1790 they rediscovered Pitcairn Island, which had been misplaced on the Royal Navy's charts. After the decision was made to settle on Pitcairn, livestock and other provisions were removed from Bounty. To prevent the ship's detection, and anyone's possible escape, the ship was destroyed and sunken. However, and now, this is where the tale gets really interesting, there was one additional item removed from the ship. It was the aforementioned piece of metal that was as light as a feather and had a low hum to it on occasion."

"There was a falling out among the men and the natives they brought with them. All but one of the white men were killed, but by this time there were many children who had been born by liaisons between the native women and the white men. Apparently, the falling out was over the fact that the white men wanted exclusive rights to the women. O.K., so they go undisturbed, living an idyllic life and Fletcher Christian's son is head man of the island. The islanders are left to live in peace for over 180 years. Today there are 48 people left on the island, all descendants of the mutineers."

Nimrod sat back and smiled, as if he was the cat that had swallowed the canary. He just sat in silence. Finally, Chablis broke the silence as she and Lynton were leaning forward, enthralled with the story but flustered that he had stopped so abruptly without an explanation of what happened to the piece of metal. "O.K., stop playing games; you know what we want to hear about."

PURSUIT

Almost laughing out loud, he said, "Ah, the piece of metal."

Nimrod motioned for the waitress, looked at Chablis and said, "It will take awhile. Mind if I have dessert?"

Frustrated, Chablis replied, "Have any damn thing you want, just finish the story."

As he waited for his double brownie fudge sundae, he continued. "O.K., so a young man who was working for the CIA is tracking various electronic signals all across the globe. You know, the CIA is always looking for something unusual that might signal a coming catastrophe for the USA, because we all know how the whole world is out to get good old America. As Bush said, 'they envy our freedom.' Talk about bullshit? I mean I worked for the CIA for 23 years and rarely saw anyone envy our freedom. They laughed at how little freedom we have. Anyway, that is another story. So, this intelligence analyst picks up a strange rumbling from of all places, Pitcairn Island. The agency sends him off to investigate. OK, so the guy lands on Pitcairn with a whole bunch of sensitive instruments to track down where this signal is coming from. The agency figures it is some terrorist group setting up operation in the South Pacific and preparing some monumental act of terrorism that will destroy that freedom everyone envies."

PURSUIT

The waitress, somewhat appalled at the appearance of Nimrod, disgustingly put the dessert in front of him. Chablis looked up at her and said, "You just blew a tip lady. You know, Howard Hughes used to dress like this guy, and looked much worse. You probably are too ignorant to know who Hughes was, but he was one of the first billionaires. Never judge a book by its cover, and never judge a person by his or her appearance. Looks can be deceiving. Like at first glance, you look like a pretty decent person, but obviously, in your case the book can't be judged by its cover."

As the waitress disgustingly left, she uttered the word bitch, to which Chablis observed, "You ain't seen bitch lady until you get me pissed."

Nimrod looked directly into Chablis' eyes and he said nothing, but you could see moisture forming in his own eyes. No matter how low he had sunk, Chablis could see the good in him, and appreciate him for the fine human being he was.

Lynton, a more reserved person than Chablis, would never have said that to the waitress, but she admired Chablis for her refusal to bow before bigotry and small-mindedness.

As he started eating his dessert with great gusto, Nimrod continued. "Anyway, this young man found something on Pitcairn that was very unusual."

J. Wayne Frye   113

Chablis could not resist. "The young man was you?"

Nodding his head, Nimrod said, "You must be a detective."

"Yep, and a good one. Go on."

"O.K., so I talk to the great, great, great, great grandson of Christian Fletcher and try to explain to him that there is an unusual electronic signal coming from the island. OK, now here is where the story takes another turn, so be patient."

"You see, a few years ago something terrible happened on the island. The remoteness of Pitcairn had shielded the tiny population from outside scrutiny. The islanders had for many decades tolerated what others classify as sexual promiscuity, even among the very young, in line with traditional values of their Polynesian ancestors and contrary to imposed Western values. This included a corresponding tacit acceptance of what is defined in as child sexual abuse. Three cases of imprisonment for sex with underage girls were reported in the 1950's. In 1999 a female police officer from the UK served a temporary assignment on Pitcairn, and began uncovering allegations of sexual abuse. When a 15-year-old girl decided to press rape charges in 1999, criminal proceedings were set in motion. The charges included rape, indecent assault, and gross indecency with a child under 14. Over the following two years, police officers in Australia, New Zealand, the United Kingdom, and Norfolk Island interviewed every woman who had lived on Pitcairn in the past 20 years, as well as all of the accused men."

Finishing his dessert, Nimrod pushed the plate aside and continued. "Now, of course, religion usually has to get involved as we all know how religious people love to impose their values on different cultures that we all know cannot compare with the high moral tone of Western Christian society. A Seventh-day Adventist pastor who spent two years on Pitcairn around the turn of the millennium, said that on his arrival, he had been taken aback by the conduct of the children who were so open about sexuality. He was further appalled to learn that Pitcairn had maintained the ancient Polynesian custom of making the age of consent 12. A study of island records confirmed anecdotal evidence that most girls bore their first child between the ages of 12 and 15. Mothers and grandmothers were resigned to the situation, as their own childhood experience had been the same; they regarded it as just a part of life on Pitcairn. One grandmother wondered what all the fuss was about. Now, I am not debating the morality of the islanders, as they live a different life in a different culture, but, although I have great disdain for the sanctimonious acts of all religion, I do think 12 might be a bit young for a young woman to have sex. Nonetheless, until Christians stop promoting war, judgemental attitudes, arrogance and forced indoctrination of children in what I consider fairy tales, I shall not look to them for any moral guidance."

Chablis and Lynton both nodded their heads in agreement as Nimrod continued. "Remember that there was a history of murder on the island also, as 13 of the original settlers were murdered. A trial was held in 2002, conducted under UK and New Zealand auspices, on the aforementioned charges, and one of those charged was a direct descendent of Christian Fletcher and town mayor."

"Pitcairn's 47 inhabitants at the time, almost all of whom are interrelated, were bitterly divided by the charges against what constituted most of the adult male population. Many Pitcairn Island men blamed the British police for persuading the women involved to press charges. Some of the women agreed. In 2004, Olive Christian, wife of the accused mayor, called a meeting of thirteen of the island's women. Claiming that underage sex had been accepted as a Polynesian tradition since the settlement of the island in 1790, Olive Christian said of her girlhood that they all thought sex was like food on the table and that the outside world had no reason to judge them by standards that did not apply on Pitcairn. Christian the 6th's two daughters also said that they had both been sexually active from the age of 14, with one of them claiming that she started having sex at 13. They and other women present at the meeting, who endorsed their view that underage sex was normal on Pitcairn, stated emphatically that all of the alleged rape victims had been willing participants."

"Now, while all this was going on, I arrived on the island and I met one of the few non-descendants of the mutineers. He had lived on the island for 50 years, and, though he was accepted by the residents, he had always felt like an outsider. He told me that there was something strange about the whole trial and that a few of the residents had secretly been attributing all their trouble to something that had been brought on the island by the mutineers, something that no one talked about until a few years before the rape charges were brought. There was a mysterious object that had been kept secure by the Christian family for years. Instantly, I knew this object was probably what was transmitting the radio signal we had picked up. Further queries simply got me a promise to meet with one of the Christian family members. She led me to a dark, dang cave on the far side of the island, where I saw the object that had for years been kept there, but a few years earlier, it had been removed for a brief time and brought to one of the Christian family homes, and that is when all the trouble started, when the accusations of child abuse made world headlines. She told me to take it, get it off the island."

J. Wayne Frye   117

PURSUIT

"The object was a piece of metal, the metal that was taken from the dinghy attached to the ghost ship the Bounty had encountered. It was as light as a feather, and on occasion, it would give off a low hum. Ladies, this item was not of this world, and I soon found it was all-powerful and seemed to have a life all its own. I found that I could communicate with it, and I will not go into detail, but what I learned scared me, made be so fearful of its power that I determined not to pass it on to the CIA. I am not Nesmond Nimrod, and I shall not tell you my real name. I have lived a life here in the Bowery for I feared what would happen if I turned that object over to the CIA. This is a nation that never uses anything for the betterment of mankind, but rather militarizes everything, even the economy, to try and subject others to our will. I finally decided that no matter what I did, the world was doomed and I along with it, so I simply gave the object to Henrietta and told her that she could turn it into a fortune. I could tell you fantastic things about its power, as it is, as I said, from another world, and in the wrong hands it can bring destruction as you never imagined possible."

Chablis, somewhat sceptical of an all powerful object from another world, said "So, I believe most of what you say, but give me an example of the object's power."

"I told you that it caused the island turmoil. It can do things, cause things to happen."

PURSUIT

"That is rubbish. An object cannot make things happen. What happened on the island was a result of years of abuse, nothing more."

Shaking his head, Nimrod was emphatic now. "Take my word Chablis, please. Until the object was brought out of that cave, the island people lived a harmonious life in obscurity and peace for close to 200 years totally shielded from the outside world. Then, suddenly, when the object was removed from the place where it had rested for nearly 200 years, people on the island began to change. Before, they were benevolent, caring, living a utopian existence. Suddenly, jealousy came into play, envy manifested itself and petty arguments broke out. It was one of these arguments which led to an older woman deciding to bring charges for being molested at 15, and in the trial, it was brought out that she had made herself willingly available to almost every man on the island. She finally recanted her testimony, but the damage had been done. The court felt compelled to make an example out of those accused. They built a special jail on the island and the men were incarcerated there for a few years, then quietly released, but the damage to the island will take generations to heal. The person who showed me the object insisted it was responsible. That it had some mystical power when it was freed from that cave and she feared that someone would once again bring it out into the light of day and the island would suffer as a result."

J. Wayne Frye   119

PURSUIT

Nimrod sighed, lowered his head and said, "O.K., I can understand why you would be sceptical, but let me share one thing with you that happened when it was in my possession, something that made me lock it away in a safety deposit box until I decided that I was going to die before long and that I should leave it with someone trustworthy, and no one was more trustworthy than Henrietta. And, of course, here I am ten years later still alive and Henrietta is dead. Anyway, I had decided that the CIA would eventually find it, because this is a nation infiltrated not by outside enemies but by enemies within. Our enemies aren't radicals in some other country that would leave us alone if we left them alone, but our enemies are right here. The government and the wealthy and the corporations that control it are our enemies."

Chablis interrupted, "I have known that since I was a little girl. Poverty is our enemy, and poverty serves the interests of the rich, so nothing is ever really done about it. However, tell me about this time when the object caused you trouble."

"O.K.," replied a somewhat invigorated Nimrod. "Many years ago, I kept the metal object in my closet. I had been hiding out for years, but I always felt the hot breath of pursuit, because I knew that the CIA never gave up. It is spending taxpayers' money, so it has no limits on how far and how long it will go in pursuit of anyone."

PURSUIT

He sighed, took a sip of water and continued. "I felt uneasiness for weeks, as I could sense that I was being followed. As I said, I had placed the piece of metal in my closet and frankly put it out of my mind. One evening I was in a terrible panic as I saw someone outside my apartment. I was on the third floor and kept looking out at two men standing by a building across the street just staring at the entrance to the building. I had been with the CIA, so I knew instantly who they were."

"I was lying on the sofa staring at the ceiling when I heard a low humming noise, and, mind you, I heard no voice, but almost telepathically, it was as if something was reading my mind. I walked over to the window, stood there staring at those men, and here is where you will think I am crazy. I simply said to myself, 'you bastards should be consumed by the fires of hell,' and in an instant they both burst into flames. I was in shock, but the humming noise got louder and my head was pounding. I knew where the noise was coming from. So, I walked to the closet and opened the door. There, on the floor where I had put it was the piece of metal glowing and pulsating. I slammed the door in fear. There were many other instances over the years when strange things happened. I admit to using its power often for a few years to keep the CIA at bay, but never for anything else. I began to learn that it could read my mind and was capable of making what I desired happen. O.K., now you think me crazy."

Lynton had dealt with the supernatural often, and was more open-minded about it than Chablis. She said, "I can understand. I have seen things that are simply not explainable. I am as much a sceptic as anyone, but I know there are just things that cannot be explained." Then she smiled and continued, "Like the poor electing Republicans to political office."

They all burst out in laughter, and Nimrod offered an astute observation. "You can always expect an American do the very opposite of what makes sense. It is the way we are programmed."

CHAPTER 6
ANSWER WRETCHES - DYING, DYING

As they walked out into the street, people were frantically listening to their cell phones as a news flash had just come across the wires of all the press associations. Chablis and Lynton whipped out their phones. A bomb had gone off in Wall Street right outside the stock exchange where the U.S. Secretary of Commerce was going to ring the opening bell to signal the start of another day of exploitation. He had been killed and 14 other well-known titans of finance who were with him had also perished. Additionally, a few dozen others had been injured. Now, of course, the Secretary of Commerce and the tycoons were all mentioned, while the lesser people were not, as money and power equals importance in the USA.

Nimrod bowed his head and said, "It has started. All hell is about to break lose."

At that moment, a shot rang out from across the street and Nimrod got an expression of complete surprise on his face as a huge hole opened up in his chest and blood began to gush out. He looked at Chablis as he began to fall toward the sidewalk uselessly trying to stem the flow of blood with both his hands, almost pleading with his eyes, not for help to live for he knew his life was over, but for help to save the nation's aggrieved people from more repression from the government.

J. Wayne Frye   123

PURSUIT

Chablis' perceptive instincts took over immediately and she quickly grabbed Lynton and pulled her behind a car as frantic people scurried about in fear. A few people were hit by shots as the shooter was obviously also trying to kill Lynton and Chablis. It was a high powered rifle, so the car was easily penetrated. Chablis looked up over the roof of the car and saw smoke coming from a third floor window in the building across the street. She took Lynton by the hand and pulled her behind a nearby van which offered more protection. Then, the shooting stopped as the shooter obviously figured he had to get out of the building in a hurry.

Chablis told Lynton to stay where she was, because she was not as experienced in dealing with these situations. Chablis artfully worked her way behind cars in the street that had been abandoned when the shooting started. She moved toward the building, and knew that the shooter would exit the rear of the building. She raced quickly toward the alley two buildings down and proceeded down it, drawing her small snub-nosed death dealer from where it was skillfully holstered in a holder attached to her inner left thigh. The alley was empty, and as she made her way toward the end, a well-dressed man suddenly appeared from the left side and was slowly and nonchalantly meandering toward the street. She shouted at him as he rounded the corner. "Hold it right there. I have a gun and I know how to use it. Freeze."

PURSUIT

He stood by the corner of the building with a smile slowly creeping across his face. "You don't want to fuck with me lady. Put the gun away or you will find yourself in some big trouble."

"Asshole, the trouble is yours. I am a vicious bitch with a dead aim. Put the hands up and don't move, not even a blink of the eyes."

"I am telling you bitch. I am government. Be cool and I will reach in my breast pocket and show you my ID."

Chablis, the gun aimed at his head, as she knew if he was a government man he probably was wearing a bullet proof vest, said, "I don't give a fuck about the government. The government is the people's worst enemy. Just freeze and we will straighten this out when the cops get here."

"Bitch, the cops will do as I tell them. I have more juice than the whole NYPD. I am telling you to let me walk out this alley and all will be OK; otherwise, you are in some deep shit."

"Been there before asshole, and always come out smelling like a rose."

He saw that he was going to get nowhere with Chablis, so he very artfully ducked behind the side of the building. Chablis knew he probably had a death dealer in his hand simultaneously as he dove behind the building. She was in the open and vulnerable, so she quickly moved to the left against the building where it would be more difficult for him to fire without exposing himself.

He very skilfully dropped to the concrete and rolled out into the open, firing upward as he knew she was probably against the building, but Chablis was one step ahead of him. She had also dropped to the pavement and when he rolled out into the alleyway firing upward, she was on the ground firing straight ahead at him, hitting him in the top of the head, ripping through it with her first bullet, spilling brains all over the concrete. Aaron had taught her to never assume anyone was dead, so always deliver a coup de grâce. She fired another bullet into the mush that had been his brain and got up and walked toward him. She put the toe of her high heel shoe under his chest and rolled him over. She reached inside his side pocket and pulled out his ID. Yep, there it was, CIA.

Chablis thought about scurrying out of the area and taking her chances, but the bullets would be matched eventually to her gun, as she was a P.I., so her gun had been test fired and the codex put in the files. She had to face the music, and it would not be pleasant. She called Lynton and told her to skedaddle. No one would probably connect her to the shooting of Nimrod. Lynton agreed, left and then Chablis called Aaron just as the police were entering the alley.

PURSUIT

Fortunately, the detective in the lead was none other than old friend John Havoc, and that pleased her immensely. He was tough, but always gave you a fair shake. He looked down at the body, then at Chablis and said, "Wherever you are, there are usually some dead bodies. Damn girl, I'd be out of work if it wasn't for you. Want to explain?"

"Was across the street with the guy this dude, in all likelihood, shot? The guy across the street is former CIA who now goes, or, I guess I should say, did go by the name of Nesmond Nimrod."

"Damn, that is some moniker. Go ahead."

Chablis took a deep breath and continued as she handed the dead man's ID to John. "This dude is also CIA as you will notice. I suppose I am in some big trouble here."

"Probably," said John as Aaron Adams stood at the alleyway entrance motioning to John, who signalled for the policeman guarding the alleyway entrance to let him come in.

As Aaron walked up, John said, "Looks like your partner is in a bit of trouble. Our government does not take kindly to CIA agents being gunned down by sexy broads packing a snub-nosed death dealer."

"Our government doesn't take kindly to much

that goes on nowadays. It prefers a complacent populace that obeys without question. Waving the flag and praying to Jesus is about all the government allows anymore."

The next thirty minutes was spent with Chablis giving details on how she wound up in the alley minus any mention of Lynton. A detective came out holding a rifle and Chablis said, "Ten to one the bullets in Nimrod will match up as being fired from that gun. Dig some of the bullets out of that car across the street and in the sidewalk, and it will match too. He not only wanted to take out Nimrod, but, for some reason, wanted to do a twofer and take me at the same time."

Pointing down at the corpse, John said, "Still doesn't mean this fellow fired the shots. Maybe he just happened to be walking through the alley."

Aaron could not resist. "About as likely as a Republican voting to increase taxes on the rich."

Three well-dressed men strolled toward John and whipped out their CIA identifications as one said, "We'll take over from here."

John, very calmly replied, "No you won't. The CIA is not sanctioned to operate in the homeland. I know you ignore the law, but I don't. Get out of the alley and get out of my investigation Mess with me, and I'll arrest you for obstruction."

PURSUIT

"You know who you messing with buddy?"

"You know who you messing with," replied John.

"You in a lot of trouble," said one of the men.

"Been in trouble before and I'm still here. Now, swivel your asses around and take a hike."

"You'll see us again, and we'll have the police commissioner with us next time."

"Hey, bring the President if you want. I will tell him the same thing. Butt out of my investigation." John turned to two uniformed policemen and said, "Escort these highly paid U.S. government boys out of the alley, and if they give you any shit, arrest their asses for obstruction."

The next several minutes were spent explaining to John about the mysterious piece of metal, but Chablis did not share the fact that she knew who had it. Anyway, John was very sceptical of any tale about a piece of metal with mystical powers.

Aaron and Chablis were thrilled that John was there, as he was a man of integrity, one of the few genuine good guys at the top who cared about people, not his career. Still, they both knew that Chablis was not out of hot water yet when he said, "You two can go, too. Don't plan on leaving town

J. Wayne Frye   129

Chablis. This looks like a righteous kill, and I'll do all I can to fend-off the feds, but I am one guy in a big department with a lot of ass-kissing suck-ups who only care about their careers, so don't expect too much out of me. However, you know you'll get a fair shake."

Aaron took Chablis by the arm and as they started to leave, he very sincerely said, "Thanks, John."

While Aaron and Chablis were tied up with the police, Lynton had turned her phone back on and finally spoken to Channa and Ingrid, who shared information about Lena Langley being at the scene of the explosion all those years ago. Lynton called Chablis with the news as she and Aaron were exiting the alley. "Thanks Lynton. Tell Channa and Ingrid they did a good job. We will go to see Lena tomorrow, and I hope we won't be shot at, but I am worried about you. Be careful, we are both now on the CIA radar and they are not the kind of people you can take lightly when it comes to the death of one of their agents."

"O.K., call me tomorrow when you are ready to see Lena."

"Will do."

Aaron hailed a cab, put Chablis in it and said, "Go home and get some rest."

PURSUIT

Every upheaval in the USA is used as an excuse to ratchet up the fear that some evil entity is lurking out there to bring the grand society that all envy to its knees. Any anarchism that brought about destruction required an immediate response from the USA, so some poor Third World country would soon be targeted as a place that needed democracy – American style. This was the way America dealt with everything, shoot first and ask questions later.

On the one hand the conservatives, who always perpetrated the conditions from whence anarchy drew its breath, namely, a wretched proletariat exploited by capital, and on the other hand, the liberals who were always fearful of being branded too peaceful and therefore were far too quick to acquiesce in repressive action were now banding together and waving the flag while appealing to Jesus to be with those who had suffered from the evil of the bad ones. So, once again, the blind American public would be willing to sacrifice sanity and common-sense at the altar of patriotic fervour.

The next day, Chablis called Lynton and arranged for a visit with Lena later in the day. Meantime, Chablis was determined to visit Roy Blount and see exactly how involved he, Hart, Swift and maybe Manly Martinez were in the recent terrorist attack. She arrived at Roy's apartment around nine in the morning, but she immediately realized something was amiss. The door was slightly ajar but she did not call out. Pushing the door slowly open she stole noiselessly into the foyer and saw two policemen and a man in plain clothes, John Havoc, standing around a large hole in the floor, and the whole apartment was strewn with pried-up planks. On the sofa, close by was a heap of bottles, gas canisters and electronic detonators.

John looked to his right, and without a word, simply using his eyes, motioned for Chablis to leave. She was in enough trouble without having to explain her friendship with Roy Blount. Instantly, undetected she glided to the door, and gently slipped out hurriedly into the street. Fortunately there was no one on watch, or her arrest would have been speedy. As it was she rapidly gained the main street and was soon lost in the broad stream of pedestrians.

Having three hours before meeting Lynton, she ducted into Starbucks, ordered a latte' and had a seat while she thought the matter over. She was furious with Roy, as it made no sense for him to get so intricately involved with a terrorist, as he was a journalist not an avid anarchist. There was only one course open to her. Outrages or no outrages, police or no police, she must find Roy. It was quite possible that Roy, ignorant of the search made at his house, might be still strolling about town, unaware of what was going on.

PURSUIT

Then, Chablis remembered a place that Roy used in emergencies just like this one. He was often in hot water and needed a place to hide out. He and Chablis were the only two who knew about it. Leaving the coffee shop, she hailed a cab, and, leaping in, ordered the driver to take her to Washington Square in Lower Manhattan. He demurred with a great swiftness when she said she was in a hurry and he whirled her swiftly on to an adventure which was to rival almost any she had ever experienced.

At the square, she dismissed the cabbie with a generous tip and walked briskly under the arch in the direction of New York University. She turned rapidly to her left and a well-known face in a cab flashed on her vision like a meteor. It was Blount, of all persons!

Shouting and waving, chasing the vehicle, she succeeded in getting it to stop. But as she approached the vehicle, she heard Roy shout, "Drive on man, drive on man. Drive on, hurry!"

Chablis, not to be denied, noticed the door was unlocked, so she grabbed the handle and opened it. "Oh no Roy, no, absolutely not."

He reached out, pulled her in and shouted to the cabbie as he did. "Get the hell outta here. Get going fast. There's a 20 in it for you. Come on, get going."

J. Wayne Frye   133

PURSUIT

Now, New York cabbies rarely argued when you offered them money, so he sped away quickly as Roy looked at Chablis and said, "You were being tailed. I thought you were a P.I."

"Sorry Roy, maybe I was not cautious. I have come to alert you. The police are on your ass."

"I know it, Chablis. I saw them at my place and never went in, got out of there as fast as I could. I am skipping out fast. The CIA has targeted me. My life isn't worth a dime. The U.S. government has me marked now."

What was the man talking about Chablis wondered. Why was he being targeted by the Central Intelligence Agency? He had the cab circle the square several times, go up town for a brief time, then back to the area near NYU when he felt they were not being tailed. He shouted for the cabbie to stop. He whispered to Chablis as he pointed to the NYU entrance. "Go through the entrance to the Psychology Building. Go up to the third floor. You will see an office with the name Dr. Ben Vivaldi on the door. Knock three times, wait three seconds, knock again, wait three more seconds and knock again. Then someone will open the door and explain everything."

"O.K. Roy, take care of yourself," said Chablis, not wanting to slow his exit since the CIA was now going to any means to get him. All she said was, "I hope you did not do it. I know you are a good guy Roy."

He shouted, "Innocent of little now, Chablis."

Suddenly, a second cab with two men in the back pulled in behind Roy and Chablis. Sensing that the people in it were far less than friendly, Chablis shouted, "Haul ass," as she grabbed Roy and they started running toward NYU.

The two guys were shocked by what happened and took a bit of time to get out of the cab and go in pursuit. Roy, as she pulled him along, suddenly got in front and emphatically said, "Follow me, Chablis."

In her foolish excitement, she obeyed him. As they rushed along she heard the men's feet pounding the pavement behind them and noticed startled on-lookers gawking at the scene. Chablis cursed her high heels and skilfully stepped out of them without missing a stride.

Once through the NYU gate, they turned left, went into some bushes and waited patiently. The two men sailed by, moving straight ahead toward the administration building, slowing down to a fast walk, looking all around. They parted company, one going into the administration building and the other going into the Communication Arts Building.

PURSUIT

Roy took her hand and deftly led her to the Psychology Building where they made their way to the office of one Dr. Ben Vivaldi. Roy performed the secret knock, but no one answered. Suddenly, they heard a noise behind them and the two pursuers stood there, revolvers drawn. They did not fire.

Half dizzy with fatigue, Chablis and Roy made a despairing sprint to the stairs on the right. She remembered that she had no gun, as hers had been confiscated by John Havoc. As she opened the door to the stairwell, she tripped and hurled violently down the first flight of stairs. All she remembered seeing was two dusky forms rushing up, and Roy hurriedly wheeling round. Then from some unknown spot broke a salvo of cracks from revolvers. A heavy body fell bleeding across her chest, and a deep dark pit opened up and swallowed her.

Where was she? She seemed to be escaping from the throes of some horrible dream, and her head was pounding mercilessly. She stretched out her right hand and it struck something cold and hard. She opened one eye with an effort, and she saw three men bending over her and she heard the sound of muffled voices. She blinked her eyes. Oh my, she wished she had not, because she assumed she was in a police cell, surrounded by three burly men who looked like they had murderous intentions.

PURSUIT

"There is not much up with your pal here," a discombobulated voice uttered.

"She just got knocked silly that's all," said Roy.

She made a supreme effort and opened both eyes fully. The light was poor, but it was enough. The face of the man nearest her was the face of Roy Blount and by him stood the old man Justin Hartman, the man from the banquet hall.

"Here, take this," said Blount, as Hartman handed him a glass of water, which he, in turn, handed Chablis.

She drank it mechanically and, imbued with new strength, bolted upright on the bench she was lying on. Blount watched here satirically as she tried to cope with the situation. By the light of a small lamp hanging in a niche over her head she saw that she was in a low small room about sixty feet square, with bare greyish-looking walls and a few slit-like openings near the ceiling. The ceiling was probably no more than a little over six feet. A few chests, several chairs, and a table of the same greyish colour constituted its furniture. Almost directly opposite her was a low door.

The three men looked extremely tall in the small room to the demure, 5:3, Chablis. She sighed a bit and shook her head as if doing so would loosen the cob webs.

PURSUIT

One of the men aroused her interest a bit when he asked if she enjoyed her run through NYU. She did not answer, as she was thinking how Roy might have made an attempt to carry her to safety. And who had fired the shots. Also, who had fallen bleeding across her chest? These and a multitude of riddles were rushing through her head.

When she had more or less fully regained voice and strength she looked at Roy and said, "Where am I?"

Roy replied, "You are in the lair of the aggrieved."

Chablis, did not fight as Roy and another man took her by the arms and lifted her up. Roy said, "You are about to see the unbelievable. However, it is only the beginning."

They moved across the room gingerly and Chablis let go of the man on her right, squeezed Roy's arm and said, "I don't need to lean on anyone but you. I don't know this asshole."

"Be very careful with your words Chablis. Mr. Swartz here is Don Hart's right hand man. It was he who stabbed one of the men pursuing you, and then very deftly clobbered the other man across the face with the butt of his gun, crushing him and instantly dispatching him to heaven or more probably hell."

PURSUIT

She nodded, and said, "I don't believe in either heaven or hell, but thanks."

They crossed the doorway and were standing in a sort of open passage which evidently ran on for some length on either side. There was a large hole on Chablis' right.

"Look below," said Blount.

She looked long and hard, while Swartz and the other man, who had given his name as Bruno, stood silently in the background. It was a strange sight, and it took a while for Chablis to seize its meaning. It was very dark outside, the only light being that coming through the doorway of the chamber she had just left, but far below in the hole glittered innumerable specks like stars. She gazed down into the depths and became aware of a low humming noise.

She squinted her eyes and there, in the hole was Don Hart, standing beside a large table, and on that table was the piece of metal – the tellurium. Horrified she said, "What is this?"

"What you are watching is a metamorphous that has been millions of years in the making. Behold what will wreck civilization and usher in a utopian society. Don is a conduit. Well, becoming a conduit that is." Roy pulled her away from the hole and continued, "I will explain."

J. Wayne Frye   139

PURSUIT

"You know about Pitcairn of course but what you don't know is that this tellurium came from the Solomon Islands. You see, there was a mighty crash in the sea there around 1775, which caused a tsunami to sweep through a smaller island. Some of the natives claimed it was a giant flying machine that crashed. More scientific analysis has postulated it was perhaps a small comet or meteor. The point is that this metal, referred to as Tellurium was for a brief period in the sea. Only two small pieces were ever brought up from the depths. Both were polished and flattened. They wound up on a merchant ship named the Polydor. That was, in all likelihood the ghost ship sighted by the HMS Bounty. It had disappeared three years prior, and it was carrying at least two pieces of the Tellurium. After the Bounty sighting, it was never seen again until 1908, when a merchant vessel rounding the Cape of Good Hope sighted it and recorded the name in the ship log. They signalled it but there was no reply as it appeared deserted. The captain was preparing to send out a boarding party, but rough seas suddenly came up and a thick fog rolled in. The next morning, when the fog had cleared there was no sight of the ship. The next sighting was in 1932, and this time there was a low hum emanating from the ship. Again, a fog came up and boarding had to be delayed. Of course, the fog lifted and the ship had disappeared. A U.S. aircraft carrier sighted it near Hawaii in 1968 as they picked up the hum on the radar. The captain was a reliable man who had never been in anyway known to panic under fire as he had been in World War II. However, when he approached the ship and saw it was empty, he ordered his men to abandon any attempt at boarding. He asked for permission to shadow the ship, but was a denied permission by Pacific Fleet Command as they thought it might be a Russian ruse to lure the ship into the open sea where it could be boarded. This was during the Vietnam War and tensions between the two nations were very high. So, there is your history of Tellurium."

Chablis looked over at Lou Swartz and said, "You believe this?"

"I believe that I love the roar of dynamite and the sound of buildings crumbling."

Roy said, "Sadist."

Swartz smiled and winked at him. He was not a terrorist with a cause. He was simply a terrorist who enjoyed killing. Chablis knew that this was a reckless man who had to be stopped, because to him, there were no innocents, only the thrill of the kill.

Then Swartz quoted Alfred Lord Tennyson: "The dynamite falls on castle walls and splendid buildings old in story. The column shakes, the tyrant quakes, and the wild wreckage leaps in glory. Throw comrade, throw: set the wild echoes flying; Throw comrade; answer wretches - dying, dying, dying."

CHAPTER 7
WHAT WE ARE FIGHTING TO ACHIEVE

Chablis was a revolutionary at heart, but she had no use for wild eyed fanatics who destroyed, maimed and killed for their own pleasure rather than in an attempt to build an equalitarian society where those at the top did not receive preferential treatment.

She felt caged in a veritable raging storm. She knew nothing of these fanatics' numbers or just what their ultimate aim was, but there seemed to be general disarray among them and no concrete plan. She knew she was pleading on deaf ears, but she could not resist saying, "Would you countenance the massacre of helpless multitudes? Is that not as tyrannical as the tyrants you want to bring down? Do you want to be like Bush and Cheney? Does it make sense to use terrorism to fight terrorism? Surely, you will only target government officials and soldiers."

"The other side has made it impossible to negotiate."

Chablis sensed a gathering horror. She felt only the helpless abject dismay with which one confronts an appalling but inevitable calamity. She believed in their cause, but surely there was another method that might avoid civilian casualties.

J. Wayne Frye   143

PURSUIT

Blount said, "You have seen that the CIA is ruthless in its pursuit of those who want justice and fairness. We don't argue here. We act boldly and with decisiveness. If you want arguments, you must wait until you see the council of five meet. They make the decisions. Disputes are resolved by their vote."

Chablis believed anarchy had its place and its purpose, but she feared these people were going to destroy their cause rather than further it. It was obviously the best policy to humour them or the result would be death for her and many more. "You used not to mind criticism," she urged Roy.

"Chablis, talk is cheap and useless. We only exist to act. Action speaks louder than words."

"Yeah, right," offered Swartz. "All these years of promises that poverty, inequity would be tackled and it is worse than ever. However, we are about to atone for all the lack of action from the wealthy and powerful. They have planted the seed of their own destruction and don't even know it."

Chablis was taken back to her cell where she looked out at twinkling lights with a terror beyond the power of words to express. All was as Roy Blount had said. The dream of Hart was going to be realized. The exile and outcast was about to come back with a vengeance. It was hot, but Chablis felt herself shivering with despair.

PURSUIT

These people had lost sight of the real cause. They now not only loathed the landlord and capitalist but the workers, whom they now saw as nothing but sacrificial lambs who had not done enough to combat their own slavery. For that, they too, were to be loathed.

Why thought Chablis had they not killed her. She was a glaring liability alive. They had wanted to make amends for the needless killing of Henrietta, but why? What good was it now that they had crossed over, crossed over into a valley of death and destruction. What was the purpose?

Blount returned with her dinner. He handed it to her and then sat down. "I am surprised you have not asked more about what happened at NYU."

Eating, she said, "Go ahead."

"It is easily told. When you fell, the two CIA operatives were up in a moment. I meant to shoot, when the agents fired two shots at me, but before I fired a shot, wam, bam out came Swartz's knife and Swift's gun butt from aloft, and both agents were killed, one spinning right across you. The explanation is that coming up the stairwell was Swartz and Swift, to whom we owe our lives. It was not part of the plan to take you, but we felt it improper to leave you in an untenable position. I am sure you are appreciative of that. I am so sorry now that I got you involved.

PURSUIT

"I am deeply involved. I already killed one CIA operative and a second and third would be a bit difficult to explain. I am thankful.

Blount got up, walked to the door and said "good night." Chablis stared at him, and felt affection and sympathy as he was trapped by circumstances. He was a victim himself, caught up in his zeal of wanting to help humanity. She said, "Good-night."

As she was dropping off to sleep she reflected on what Lena and Lynton would think of her absence. No doubt, they were worrying.

It was late the next morning, when the blurred imagery of her dreams mingling strangely with the memories of the preceding night, she awakened to reality. She began, as she rose from the hard bed, to meditate on how to get out of a predicament that, no doubt, was one of the most tenuous situations she had ever been in. She grinned and shrugged her shoulders, thinking that all things considered, it was just one life in the sea of plenty. Still, the apprehensions of the past night had given way to a hopeful spirit, while the interest of exploring what these people planned was actually motivation enough to try and stay alive. Anyway, death had never scared Chablis, because it came to everyone. The only thing frightful about dying to her was the suffering that most people must endure before the end.

PURSUIT

Suddenly, in walked Roy, saying "Get up woman, Mr. Don Hart wants to see you."

Roy stood there staring as Chablis looked over at the sink, thinking she should tidy herself up just a bit. She grimaced at Roy and said, "You mind letting a lady get cleaned up in private?"

"Well, I had rather watch. You know I have always wondered what you looked like naked."

"Like any other girl except for what is between my legs. Hey, half the men in Manhattan have seen me naked anyway. I am a very promiscuous girl. You want to watch, go ahead, but let a lady at least use the toilet in private."

"Done," he said as he got up and closed the door behind him.

It took Chablis about 20 minutes to get ready, and while she was doing so, Roy was talking to her through the opening in the door. Chablis said, "You got any clothes around her that might fit me? What I am wearing is pretty dirty. Men's clothes are fine, just as long as they are clean."

"Yeah, Lou is a small guy. I will see what I can do. Don't forget your promise. I finally get to see you naked."

"Hey, a promise is a promise."

PURSUIT

He was gone for awhile, and Chablis finished cleaning up, standing under the seldom used shower just letting the water cascade over her dark and soft, luscious skin. There was no shame in Chablis. She looked down at her taunt body and realized she had been graced with what could at the very least would be described as a bombshell of a body. Everything was absolutely perfect about it, but what was between her legs, and for some men, that was even a grand allure that titillated something in them they did not understand. Forbidden fruit, the out-of-the-ordinary were what made life interesting.

It must be understood that sex is like an aphrodisiac of the mind more than the body. The situation Chablis found herself in was fraught with danger, but at that very moment, she felt a stiffening of her member as she looked around the prison that was now her home, thinking that she had never had sex in such a dirty place. She felt her sphincter muscle relax as she wondered if Roy was packing a big one that he could shove deep into her and titillate her soul. Damn, she was really hot.

She stood there naked by her cot, and when Roy walked in with some clothes in his hands, he just stood there in awe of the most incredible woman's body he had ever seen. It was as if Michelangelo had taken chisel in hand and sculpted an absolute masterpiece.

PURSUIT

Chablis had artfully stuck her now soft member down between her legs and no one could tell that she was not a genetic woman as the generous pubic hair could be mistaken as covering a grand and glorious pussy. Of course, most American women had long ago fallen for the marketing hype of the adult magazines, *Playboy* in particular, which had promoted the shaved pube look. Chablis, had never fallen for the marketing hype, and men seemed to get excited seeing a woman who was independent thinking enough to not fall prey to the Madison Avenue hype.

Roy was almost shaking with excitement as he turned and bolted the door, tossing the clothes and the shoes he had procured onto the cot as he said, "Goddamn, never in my life Chablis, never have I seen anything more beautiful."

Giving him a devilish smile, she very provocatively said, "Do something about it then."

He swept her in his arms and as their tongues were furiously duelling in a dance of delight, Chablis artfully began to undress him. Pulling his pants off and looking at his member trying to pop through his briefs, she quickly freed it and dropped to her knees as she was delighted to see it was the size of a giant cucumber. She devoured it like a champ in one smooth swallow, burying it into the back of her throat, much to the delight of Roy.

PURSUIT

It has been said that when you are lucky enough to have your member in Chablis' mouth it is as if you have hooked it up to a high powered vacuum cleaner that will suck the very life out of you. Roy was moaning and breathing like a long distance runner who had just finished a marathon. He was telling himself that he was on the verge of a heart attack, but if it happened, what the hell, he would go with a big smile on his face.

Now, when most men cum it is a feeling of euphoria that only lasts a few seconds, but with Roy this time, it was like a grand symphony in Carnegie Hall with the kettle drums pounding on and on. He fervently gushed his liquid elixir of pleasure forth like water cascading over Niagara Falls and pounding into the whirlpool below. His member pumped and pumped in what seemed like a never ending explosion that slammed the back of Chablis throat as she guzzled every last drop like it was water in a pond in an oasis that she had come upon after days of dryness in the desert and she could not satiate her thirst until every last drop was devoured. She moaned with pleasure as his liquid kept pumping out and slammed the back of her throbbing throat.

Finally, his member completely emptied, she, keeping it in her mouth as it slowly diminished in size, tilted her eyes upwards and they were twinkling with delight that she had so thoroughly satisfied him. She swelled with pride that she was the most prolific, perfectly skilled cock sucker to ever have a man's member in her mouth.

She slowly got up from her knees and wrapped her arms around Roy, looking up at him with a great sense of accomplishment splashed across her beautiful brown face. She whispered, "If you liked that baby, I got something for you that was designed by God to bring men pleasure they never dreamed possible."

Then, she let go of him, turned around, leaned over on the cot as she tucked her knees under her, propping her ass high in the air and wiggling it as she placed her face to the side of the cot, reached back with both hands and pulled apart her cheeks. "Moisten it up baby and get ready to ride the merry-go-round of pleasure."

For Chablis, the rear hole had always been her pussy, and as such, it was so wide open that Roy wondered if he could not get his whole face in the opening. He licked around it to moisten it up as he felt his member grow larger and larger, anticipating what a delight it would be to pound on that monument to pleasure.

Knowing that verbalization excited men, Chablis said, "Fuck it baby. Come on, fuck it hard, please. I need it so bad, baby. I need to have you dump a load of your hot, steamy, beautiful white liquid joy juice inside me."

PURSUIT

In an instant, Roy had his member shoved up into Chablis so far that he felt like he was in a gold mine and had just hit the mother lode. Now, sex is more in the mind than the body, but the mind controls the body, and Roy's mind was making his body into a fine-tuned pounding machine as the furiousness of his ramming in and out was like a piston in an engine that was honed to absolute precision. There was complete perfection as Roy's piston worked Chablis cylinder of love.

Chablis worked her sphincter muscle to perfection, squeezing his member as if she needed his joy juice to keep breathing. It was what gave her life. Suddenly, with a mighty shove, Roy drove his member so far up into her cavity that Chablis felt like the tip of his joy stick was actually tickling her throat. He exploded like a box of TNT that had just had a match light a short fuse. The liquid rammed out into her cavity and she moaned with pleasure, feeling that she was all woman all the time and that the pleasure she brought men was the crowning glory of her womanhood.

Thoroughly alive to the situation, Chablis lay there naked for awhile just breathing heavily as Roy lay down on the cot beside her, exhausted and spent of all energy. Chablis reached over and started putting on the men's clothes that Roy had brought. Looking at her get dressed, he said, "It is a sin to cover up that body."

PURSUIT

Chablis, laughing, said "Of course it is, but I can't do this all day, and if I don't get dressed I will be sucking and fucking constantly. A girl needs a little rest now and then."

She had no idea what lay ahead for her. Was that to be her last sex act? Oh, it had been so good. Was she going to be sacrificed at the altar of expediency? Was she preparing to be another victim of anarchy?

As they walked out of the cell into a hallway and made their way down toward a stairwell, Chablis wondered just how many men there were there. She saw a few standing around, and wondered what the plan was. Something big was brewing, and it all revolved around that crazy piece of metal.

"You know Chablis, you think that the core of this enterprise is Don Hart, and he is, indeed an integral part of what makes things work, but sometimes great things are accomplished by those who plan while the actions are carried out by the more physically bold. You are about to get a surprise."

They walked through double doors into a large dormitory filled with men and a few women who were obviously from varied ethnic groups. They all looked up at Chablis, but one man, who was sitting at the head of a dining table, had a huge grin on his face. He did not say a word, just pointed to a chair to his right, indicating Chablis should take a seat.

She was only mildly shocked at who the man was, but she was surprised to see a man his age who was obviously the head of the band of anarchists who had a lair somewhere in New York City, hidden from the prying eyes of those who would question their motives.

As she sat down, Justin Hartman said, "Surprised to see an old anarchist like me heading up this band of miscreants?"

"I am up to a point, but it actually is not all that shocking. That night at the banquet, you were obviously a man filled with anger about the state of affairs in this nation. However, I did not know you had used all those years in jail to plan the rise of anarchy and the destruction of the society of greed."

With a twinkle in his eyes, Justin Hartman offered a profound retort. "I am not vain enough to compare myself to Nelson Mandela, who suffered 28 years of incarceration for trying to bring equality to the Blacks of South Africa, but he knew that you won nothing by bowing before the slaveholders. He was a man of peace who realized that violence was the only way to make the whites come to the conference table. Enduring torture and loneliness for so many years, I postulated plans with people like Hart, Swift, Martinez and Swartz, preparing for a day of atonement for all who have suffered at the hands of evil. It was a highly clandestine communication between all of us that lay plans for a day when we would find the way to finally destroy a society that is an abomination to compassion and love. I had no idea I would be freed and that a secret weapon would fall into our hands that would tip the scales so heavily in our favour."

"Are you sure of this enterprise? Do you not feel that there are elements here who just want to destroy, not build?"

Hartman glanced at Swartz who was standing in a corner talking to another man. "I know that there are elements here who are less than stellar in their devotion to the cause, but it takes ruthless people sometimes to carry out plans that, in the end, will foster the dawn of hope for those who have waited far too long to be embraced with compassion and offered a hand up rather than given the back hand of disdain. You are an admirer of Che, so you know he could be ruthless when it was called for."

Chablis sighed, knew she could not persuade Hartman to take another route, but still offered her heartfelt opinion. "You killed a lot of people in Wall Street the other day, including some innocents. What did that accomplish?"

PURSUIT

"That was not my intention – to kill innocents. We want to avoid that at all costs. The reason we wanted you to find Henrietta Hobson's children was to show our compassion, to prove to the world that when we make mistakes we are willing to atone for them. Now, the explosion on Wall Street was the first salvo in a war of attrition. The aim was to kill the Secretary of Commerce, who is supposed to represent the small businessman but who only represents the corporations. Where did he come from? What qualified him for his job as Secretary of Commerce, being a Wall Street banker, of course? The Secretary of Commerce should not come from the industry he is regulating. For far too long, the fox has been let loose in the hen house."

"So, you are about to unleash, with the help of that piece of mysterious metal that is so important to you and the CIA, the festival of the oppressed, and, in the end, you think the oppressed will rise up? Forget it Hartman. The people have become so complacent they have lost the will to fight. They just want their cable or satellite television with the most inane entertainment imaginable, their smart-phone with all the latest gadgets and a trip to McDonald's for a burger and fries. That is the way they are mollified into complacency. Believe it or not, many people think that is the good life. What they don't realize is that they have all been made slaves. However they no longer care, Hartman."

"Our secret weapon is being perfected at this moment while we speak. That piece of metal is going to be the key that opens the door to revolution. To avoid discovery, we have taken every precaution, and right now three beacons of enormous power are being perfected. We are on the verge of tipping the scales in favour of the little guy for a change."

Chablis was fascinated now. "You have a secret weapon?"

He took her by the hand, led her out of the dining hall and as they proceeded down a hallway, he said, "You have seen Hart communicating with that hunk of metal. It is capable of incredible things. We are now forging an instrument of destruction no one has ever envisioned. Come and behold man's salvation."

They entered into the lower part of that hole she had peered into previously and there was Hart sitting at a large round table. Justin said, "Behold Chablis, our instrument of retribution. This is the man destined to lead us into the age of enlightenment."

Hart, very calmly got up, walked over to Chablis and said, "You have been fortunate to have been privy to all this knowledge and allowed to live. Roy says you are a woman of integrity and would never betray us, but I am not so sure. I think you have a soft spot for the moneyed class. I believe your compassion makes you suspect."

In complete awe, Chablis looked at the grand and glorious sight. There, on that table before her was an instrument that was sealing the fate of humanity. Was it for the good she asked herself? Should she join in earnest these people who were so devoted to an ideal? She began to visualize what it would be like to sail effortlessly through life in a utopian world where all had shelter, food, a job, hope. What was this weapon they were talking about? The piece of metal had no destructive power that she could see.

As they walked around the table, Justin said, "I know you are wondering where its destructive power is hidden?" Then he pointed at three small objects beside the piece of metal, "That is the key. The piece of metal telepathically communicates. It sent us to a place in the Solomon Islands where the three beacons were hidden. We brought them back, and the power they possess is not of this world."

"I still don't see how this is going to change the equation," said Chablis.

"Ah, the finishing touches are being completed dear Chablis. We shall take you for a test of the new world this afternoon. Believe me, what we have is going to change the equation and put power in the hands of the oppressed for a change. Go back to your cell, rest and prepare for the ride of your life – a better ride than sex."

Hart excused himself, leaving Justin and Chablis there alone. Despite the seriousness of the situation, Chablis could not help but laugh. Justin knew. Yes, he knew that she and Roy had sex that morning. She gave him a wink, and through a half laugh, replied, "Ask Roy if this object and all it portends is better than sex."

Justin, immensely attracted to Chablis, said "Why don't you show me just how good sex with you is?"

"Why Justin, you dirty old man."

"Take me back to your cell, and I will show you just how dirty."

She took his hand and whispered softly as they walked toward her cell, "I am going to give you the best butt you ever had old man. However, I have a surprise between my legs that might shock you."

"Chablis, everyone knows you are a transsexual. Remember, I have been in prison where you get more sex than anywhere else, and the sex I have had for ten years has not been exactly conventional, but I can say without hesitation, you are a woman. I know that and anyone in the world with a grain of intelligence that has not been infected with religion, knows that what is between your legs does not define gender."

As they went into her cell, Chablis almost laughed. Who would have imagined she would have so much sex in this place?

Justin was a bit nervous, but Chablis said, "Don't worry, let's shower and prepare for love."

He was overwhelmed at the magnificent body that he shared the shower with. As he watched the water cascading over her dark brown soft skin his old member got as hard as a baseball bat. Chablis lathered it up with soap and began to work it back and forth. It was an old one, but it was a big one, she noticed much to her delight.

Sex is, if one gives it close scrutiny, not much more than a recreational activity. However, with Chablis, it was a recreational activity of the highest and grandest order. She liked Justin, and decided that she was going to give this old man a thrill he would remember on his death bed. She led him to the cot and had him lie down, his member pointing straight to the ceiling like a flagpole that was flying the flag of carnal joy flapping in an erotic breeze. Ah, and Chablis was going to salute his flag with a warm, inviting mouth that devoured his member and swallowed it all the way to its hairy base where she buried her nose and smelled the erotic odour of his dark and grey-speckled pubic hair which titillated her. She eased off very slowly working her way with a sucking motion toward the tip of his joy stick. Then, just as she got almost to the head she swiftly swept back downward to the base again, swallowing it with gusto. Back and forth, back and forth she went relentlessly as he gleefully sighed.

Chablis had often wondered why she loved doing that so much, and ultimately she realized it was her power-trip. Yes, she exalted in the power she had over men with the way she used her mouth, and then when she offered them ass, they went wild. So, for her, it was not about the physical feeling, but rather, the psychological feeling of power that it conveyed upon her.

Justin was totally silent except for satisfying moans of pure delirium. As Chablis felt him tensing up and ready to explode, she artfully backed off, grabbed his stiff member, straddled him and skilfully glided it into her gapping hole as she whispered, "You are going to douse my hot fire of desire with your long, hot fire hose that will squirt your liquid fire extinguishing load deep inside me, baby."

If she had been a jockey in the Kentucky derby, she would have been atop a winner, as she road his member furiously as if the devil himself was chasing her and only Justin's hard cock was keeping her from being caught. Justin began to thrust upward, meeting each downward stroke, and Chablis worked her sphincter muscles, squeezing, squeezing his member as if each squeeze was a plea for the liquid that would finally put out her raging fire. She let out low guttural sounds and began to beg for his liquid. "I need it baby. Come on; pump me full of that hot throbbing joy juice that I crave."

Justin let out a mighty roar that shook the ceiling and rattled the walls as he gushed a river of joy juice into Chablis, who moaned ecstatically with each pulsation of his hot member. When he had emptied every last drop, she squeezed again and again to make sure she had all of it inside her.

The loud noises had aroused suspicion, and walking through the door Roy stood in shock at the two naked people before him. Chablis was still astride Justin, but she pulled herself off his hot flag pole that was now at half mast and there was a slight swishing noise as her cavity closed back up. She turned and smiled at Roy as she said, "Good stuff must be shared. Remember, you want equality of opportunity for all. I am a girl who is an equal opportunity fucker."

Justin, quickly started getting dressed, but Chablis had never had any shame about her body, so she just lay there naked, not covering herself up, as Roy said to Justin, "we are ready to make a test of the weapon if you have any energy left."

Justin, somewhat proud of his accomplishment for an old man, replied, "Never felt more alive in my life," then he looked down at Chablis, smiling as he said, "And this is the reason for it. Thank you Chablis."

Chablis gave him a wink and said, "Remember me in your will."

Chablis asked if she was invited to see the weapon's test. Roy and Justin both nodded in the affirmative, but Roy could not resist, "Only if you promise not to fuck all the people working on the project."

Chablis smiled and replied, "Had the two best fucks around here already, everything else would pale in comparison."

Roy said, "Put your damn clothes on and let's go."

What was before Chablis, as she entered the room with maybe 10 others in single file, were the three beacons and the pulsating piece of metal. Roy, Don Hart, Bob Swift, Manley Martinez and Lou Swartz stood by the table. Justin, along with Chablis, stood in a far corner. Don said, "Let there be quiet please. He then motioned for Bruno to open the curtain at the far end of the room. There was a huge metal cage, and in the cage was a snorting pig, pacing back and forth. Don picked up one of the beacons and aimed it toward the metal cage. It began to pulsate and hum.

The piece of metal also began a low hum and there seemed to be a slight emission of light between it and the beacon. Don pointed the beacon directly at the pig and in a split second, the pig and cage had disintegrated into dust. Everyone present gasp and Roy walked over to where the cage and pig had been. He waved his hand over the area where the cage had been. Nothing was there, nothing, only a pile of dust.

"Molecular disassembly," said Don. "The molecules have disappeared, dissipated back into tiny atoms. The. military would use this weapon to bring the world to its knees, but we have it. We have the means to finally effectuate change."

There was a light in Don's eyes, a glow of assurance that he could now accomplish his noble goals of a utopian society. However, when Chablis looked over at Swartz, she felt trepidation. There was something not right about the sinister look on his face, some key to the door of evil was now near his hands. To him, this was power, raw power that he now had access to. Hart walked over to Chablis. He took her by the hand and said, "Come with me."

PURSUIT

They ascended a spiral staircase to the upper part of the room. Glancing hastily around, Chablis saw they were on an upper deck that looked over the room below. Don Hart sighed.

Chablis had never even tried to figure out where she was, but suddenly, she wondered if there was a way she could escape to the surface above, because she saw a faint light that appeared to be coming through the narrow windows at the top of the deck, maybe 12 feet above. She could make out, looking upward, an exterior wall at least 30 feet high, surmounted with spikes, and having an almost deathly grey look to it. Sullen, isolated, and menacing, it overwhelmed her with a vague premonitory dread. Hart strode up a door nearby and pressed a knob. She heard the ting of an electric bell and the door swung open. Hart said, "Walk down the hallway with me, and you will meet someone familiar."

Chablis, mastering some natural excitement, walked through the inner portal and found herself in a narrow hall. Flights of steps were straight ahead and the two descended them until they came to a landing where there were doors on the right and left. The one to the left was half open and her escort motioned for her to enter and, pulling the door open, she was shocked to see sitting behind a desk a smiling, a well-dressed, extremely handsome man of maybe forty-five. She had enjoyed a tryst with him several times, and as they stared at one another, she wondered if Mac McAllister had been setting her up for this the last time they had a rendezvous in her apartment. Still, he looked different now. A straight piercing gleam in his eye made him appear harsher.

The impetuous air that had attracted Chablis seemed to have given way to a cold inflexible sedateness. As she advanced into the room, he rose, a grand specimen of manhood, standing tall and stately. He walked around the table, embraced her warmly and motioned tacitly toward a seat.

"I am glad to see you again. The last time was very memorable."

Smiling, and glancing over at Hart, knowing he must comprehend what the innuendo was, she said, "Yes, most memorable it was."

She felt he was weighing her fate in his mind. He had a contemplative look as he said, "So, you have been a busy girl since last I saw you, but I want to thank you for finding the Hudson girls. We will render them compensation for their loss. Ironic isn't it that even we socialists think money can compensate for the death of someone. No matter what, it appears that in the end everything comes down to dollars and cents."

"In a world," said Chablis as she shrugged her shoulders, "where we're taught the good life can be bought, what would you expect? I like to think I have integrity, but if offered compensation for the death of a loved one, I would take it. Why not? The loved one is still dead regardless. Better to have something than nothing."

"You are a realist Chablis – an idealist, but still a realist. So, what do you think about what is going on here?"

"I am lost in wonder. But I am also fearful of what you all are pondering to do with the new found knowledge you have acquired. Those whom you have already killed haunt my conscience as you contemplate more destruction in the future, and the purpose of those beacons whose power I have seen bothers me."

He listened without comment as a man possessing his power could well afford to be tolerant. Looking directly into her eyes, he said, "Do generals dissolve into tears when they lose men in battle? Do they shrink from the wholesale slaughter which every campaign entails? I am a general here, along with Hart, and we cannot cry because some people must die. It is the way of war, and we are at war here. We are at war against the vast forces of darkness represented by the wealthy and powerful who sit on their thrones of gold expecting all of us to bow before them and grovel for a few crumbs from their tables of plenty. There comes a time when you must get off your knees and stop begging for what is rightfully yours."

Chablis, always filled with compassion for the innocents, said, "In your war you are not against a defined army, but against society as a whole, and you are bringing the innocent down with the guilty. I support your ideology, but slaughtering the innocent only puts you on the same level as the people you abhor. It is like Bush and Cheney justifying terror to fight terror. Look what that has got the world."

"There is a difference Chablis between what we want and what those war criminals wanted. There's was a war for conquest of the world for corporations and a system of economic servitude. We seek to free man of servitude, to elevate him to a higher plain where each person is valued and not looked upon as a commodity to be exploited so the few can lead lives of grandeur. Can you not see that all the great movements for change used brutal methods to usher in tranquility? Che was the most completely compassionate man who ever drew the breath of life, but he saw that brutality was all the privileged class understood. He lined the exploiters up against a wall and dispatched them with no remorse, because he knew you had to eradicate them for all time or their insidious greed would infect a new generation. The Bolsheviks knew that they had to eradicate the Czar and his entire family, because as long as the royal line existed the very people they oppressed would still bow before those they somehow thought superior by virtue of birth. The mind is easily manipulated. Most people want others to do their thinking for them. That is why we must destroy apathy as well as the privileged class."

"Mac, you are justifying the absolutely unjustifiable. That prick Cheney went on for years with his puffed out chest and arrogant pontificating. He believed any crime was justifiable if you just used the term national security. No matter what he said, in the end, there was no justification for him and that buffoon Bush killing so many innocents."

"Can you not see Chablis that the victory in view is the regeneration of man? The cost will be some thousands, perhaps hundreds of thousands or millions of lives, but in the end, humanity can be saved from those rich, arrogant, self-serving bastards."

Chablis, very thoughtfully replied. "Certainly the ideal is a grand one, and might, if reliable, be worth the outlay. But how many of your crew appreciate its truth or really understand what they are fighting for? I have seen the look in Swartz's eyes when he talks about death and blowing things up. He obviously enjoys destruction for its own sake. He is not an aide, but a danger to your cause."

"Every man here is an outlaw from society in one way or another, and most have shed blood. They long to wreck revenge on society for the evils which they have received, or, given the appropriate occasion, would receive. In this endeavour, we must embrace all who offer devotion to our cause."

Chablis sighed, "But Mac, just because someone is secure, resolute, fiery and unflinching in devotion does not mean he or she is going to make a good soldier. Look at all the American soldiers sent into foreign lands. They don't garner respect for America. With their swaggering arrogance, they foster further hatred. You have some soldiers who are going to do the same."

"Don't worry Chablis. I know how to control my soldiers and so does Don. "

"I hope so Mac. You know, I really like you. That is why I went out with you in the first place, but I had no idea you were such a fervent believer in violent revolution. You kept it hidden well."

Mac motioned for Hart to take her out. He said lovingly, "Take care of this lady, Don. She is more than just a beautiful woman. She represents the heart and soul of what we are fighting to achieve."

PURSUIT

CHAPTER 8
ONLY SLIGHTLY BETTER

"One more question" Chablis said to Hart as they walked down the hall. "How do you propose to destroy the moneyed class now that you have that infernal piece of metal and those beacons?"

"I cannot say much as yet. But, understand, the day when the first bomb falls will witness outbreaks and uprising of the people who will demand an end to the madness of capitalism. We are much stronger than we seem. We have adherents in every great city in Europe. We have hundreds in New York City alone and many more scattered across the nation. While the government is busy worrying about Muslim terrorists we are building a network that will bring an end to real terrorism – the terrorism of capitalism. When the revolution starts, no one will know what hit them. During the tempests of bombs, those awaiting our signal will fill the streets in all directions, rouse up the populace, and let loose pandemonium upon earth. In the confusion, due to our attack, order and precautions will be impossible. This is the dawn of a new age.

"You scare me Don. Do you really believe this will work? You will only wreck civilization, not save it. The result of this will be folly as you would never imagine. I am all for revolution, but systematic and orderly revolt."

PURSUIT

"There will be a new order, Chablis."

"But how is the new order to take shape? How do you rise from the chaos?"

Hart was becoming emphatic now. "We want no more systems or constitutions. Men will abjure the foulness of the modern wage-slavery and a system of equality shall rise."

"Are you dreaming, Hart? Chaos means a new ruling class will arise to take the place of the old one. I am a socialist, you know, but I have felt how selfishness and the risks of reaction hampered our most promising plans all over the world. Americans believe that Hollywood buffoon, Ronald Reagan, drove the nail in the coffin of the true socialist nation, the Soviet Union, with his insane defence expenditures, but it was the Soviet system itself that caused its own demise. They lost the vision of hope and let class stratification creep into the system, making it no different than capitalism. The ruling class became like the rich in this country, never having enough for themselves while denying sustenance to millions."

Don said, "I cannot argue points of revolt with you. The die has been cast. All we want from you is to get the money for compensation to the Hudson sisters and make sure it is publicized so that the country can know we have a heart, and that we are not unfeeling and uncaring."

PURSUIT

Chablis knew that Don's heart was in the right place. All he wanted was for mankind to reach its full potential unimpeded by greed which was so central to the worst economic system ever devised. She looked at him in earnest as she said, "I believe in your devotion to the betterment of mankind. Truly I do, and I want the same thing you do, but above all I want to avoid bloodshed."

"Chablis, blood is the purifying element that washes away the old order. Only with the spilling of the blood of the oppressors is the revolution sanctified."

"I cannot," seriously retorted Chablis, "support unequivocal violence, though I can sanction its precise implementation against the oppressors. I am not going to reveal what I know to anyone but perhaps my partner Aaron Adams who is as loyal and dependable an ally to the working man as am I, for I have loyalty to my clients and you are, in a crazy sort of way, all my clients. However, when my clients cross the line between good and evil, I must always ere on the side of good. I hope you understand that? I see much good here. What I don't see is a check on one element here that I see as loose cannons. I worry about Swartz and his pal Bruno as lose screws in a well-oiled machine of revolution. You must be extremely vigilant against any breech of propriety toward a noble cause with noble goals. You are only as strong as your weakest links."

J. Wayne Frye   173

PURSUIT

"We know there are weak links yes, and we are also perplexed about something else that has manifested itself of late. My father is a man of integrity, and he has suffered immeasurably because first, he had a son whose homosexuality was an embarrassment for him among his social set, and, of course, because I fouled up and killed an innocent bystander unintentionally. Of course, for most people, that was secondary to the fact that I was, according to the media, a bomb-making, ranting, anti-social psychopathic homo. But now Chablis, I want to make amends." He handed her a bank book. "The money is there for the two sisters, all my personal fortune, $323,000. I want their names and I will arrange for the Swiss bank to transfer it an account I will arrange for them. Give it to them and say that though I can never be forgiven for what happened, I want them to know that I am truly sorry."

Chablis reached into her pocket where she had put the names earlier for safe keeping and handed him the names of the two women. "I will expect the transfer right away and will arrange it as you want."

"You see things well, Chablis. There are those here who do not want you freed for fear you might somehow figure out where you were held and alert the authorities to our hiding place. One word now, Chablis, I ask you neither to join us nor to agree with us. You are your own master. All I ask is that you be honourable. Give me your word as a person of honour that you shall not reveal our location, and I shall arrange your flight from this place."

"You have my word up to a point. As I said, you are my client, and until the job is finished I am honour bound to you. Once the two women pick up the money though, our professional arrangement is over, so I suggest you retain me for another job that might be beneficial to you."

"What job?"

"You know Lena Langley?"

"I do, or did many years ago. What about her?"

"My co-investigators discovered something very unusual in a photograph taken at the place where the bomb went off that day. After you had scurried away with that mysterious hunk of metal, when the crowd was milling around, there near the cart stood Lena Langley. Any connection between you two?"

A perplexed Don replied, "Absolutely not. Ah, I get your drift. I hire you to explore her connection to this whole affair and we have a client-investigator privileged relationship, which, of course, insolates you from any criminal intent. Smart woman you are. So, how about a one dollar retainer. After giving the girls all that money, I am broke."

Smiling, Chablis replied, "Well, I was going to say fifty cents, but hey, I might as well get rich, uh?"

He reached in his back pocket and brought out his billfold. It was empty of cash. So, Chablis reached in her pocket, pulled out a five dollar bill, handed it to him and said, "A loan. Now pay me the retainer. Let's make it five dollars."

They laughed and headed down the hallway. Still it preyed upon Chablis' mind that there was such an abyss of difference between Don, whom she had obviously misread when she sensed a sinister element within him at Roy's house and Swartz, who with his friend Bruno, seemed to be more enthralled with destroying things than building a just society.

At that point, Swartz and Bruno came down the hallway from behind them, approaching the two. Swartz said excitedly, "We fear our location has been compromised, this bitch has sown mistrust in the ranks."

Don, very determined said, "This woman sows no discord. She is only interested in the welfare of those we might hurt as we try to instil a new order in the world."

PURSUIT

Swartz reached into his vest pocket and pulled out a gun. "We all had a vote. Everyone but Roy says ice the bitch."

From behind Swartz and Bruno, Chablis saw Roy slowly edging up the hallway in their direction. She had learned long ago from Aaron that when you had a gun in your face, you don't waste time negotiating; you make a move to protect yourself. Without hesitation she pivoted on her left foot, raising her right one and kicked Swartz in the balls, balanced a bit lower and pivoted right to do the same to Bruno. Swartz's gun slid across the floor, but there was no time to pick it up. As Roy rushed forward, he picked it up and the three of them sailed down the hallway like a flock of geese scared by the report of a gun.

Made a big mistake thought Chablis as she turned the corner with the two men. Aaron always said that if you leave an adversary breathing, you have a problem. She knew she should have taken the gun from Roy and pumped Swartz and Bruno full of lead. Roy pointed toward a metal door to the left and said, "He was not completely accurate, about everyone agreeing to ice you, Chablis." then he turned toward Don Hart and said, "Manley is waiting outside with a car ready to roll. We are all hauling ass out of here. Your dad has a plane waiting at Teterboro Airport."

"Ah," said Chablis. "We're in Jersey."

PURSUIT

Realizing that Chablis recognized the name Teterboro, Roy said, "Right, but it won't do any good to know, they are already packing up and getting ready to leave this place. I am afraid, Chablis, that we all threw in with the wrong group of anarchists. This is not about revolution to free the masses from the wealthy tyrants anymore. It is about revolution to replace one group of tyrants with another. Those two we left lying on the floor are sadistic bastards who just want to blow things up and people along with the things. They are psychopaths of the first order, I am afraid."

"Good intentions can attract bad people," said Chablis. "I still believe in your goals."

Don Hart, as they ran out the door to a nearby car, said to Chablis, "You are a wise woman."

The engine was racing and the three piled in the car with Manley. He roared off into the night as Chablis and Roy, sitting in the back seat, looked out the rear window and saw lights coming on all around the compound. Chablis said, "You can slow down. They are too smart to pursue us. They are getting out of that place as quickly as possible. We have some big decisions to make, and I need to know what you want now, so I can make appropriate plans."

Manley, looking in the rear view mirror at Chablis, said, "We won't to stay out of jail."

PURSUIT

Smiling, Chablis said, "O.K., I will keep your names out of this. I believe you have all been duped by a group that only wants anarchy, not revolution. You all know you can rely on me, but the U.S. government is not above torture. For that reason, in case they incarcerate me and sweat me, I don't want to know where you are. Under torture I might not be so reliable. You guys take that plane to wherever, but only get in touch with me daily. Call me daily at different phone booth. Every day I will put the contact number in the morning classifieds of the *New York Times*. I will reverse the number, so 123456789, becomes 987654321. Call me at 6 PM every day at the number. If I don't answer, try every hour until midnight. O.K.?

"What are you going to do Chablis," asked Don.

"I am going to get to the bottom of all this. There is something very sinister going on here. First, I want to know why Lena was at the scene of that bombing ten years ago. Second, I want to know why the C.I.A. keeps popping up everywhere. I also want to know the real story of Nesmond Nimrod and why he was a target for assassination. I am on this case to the end, and in the end, there may be some ass kicked by yours truly."

Don said to Chablis, "and don't forget the money to the girls. This does not change doing an

J. Wayne Frye   179

act of contrition to make up for my mistake. Take care of that also, please, but you can forget publicizing it. That is no longer necessary. "

"Will do," Chablis said as she motioned for Manley to stop. "I will get out here and hitch a ride back to Manhattan. You guys go wherever, and hide out. We will be in touch."

They all nodded in agreement and Roy said, "You're a hell of a woman, Chablis."

Chablis winked at Roy and said, "Hell of a cock-sucker, too," as she slammed the door and stood by the road with her thumb out.

Seeing Chablis hitch-hiking almost caused a wreck as men were slamming on breaks to stop and pick her up. Two tractor trailers, three cars and a pickup all stopped by the roadside, and Chablis simply asked the guy nearest her, the one in the pick-up, if he was going to Manhattan. He said, "Lady, I am going to L.A. if that is where you are headed."

Laughing, Chablis said, "Manhattan will do just fine."

She crawled in the pickup cab, much to the chagrin of the others who had stopped. The guy looked over at her, took a deep breath and said, "Damn, this old pick-up ain't been this lucky since never."

Chablis said, "You're cute. Play your cards right and you and the pick-up might get lucky."

"Lady, the way I feel right now I'm holding a royal flush."

The trip back took them over the GW and the two of them it off great. He was 21, in school at Hunter College and earning extra money by hauling scrap metal to the New Jersey dump. He asked her where she wanted to be dropped off, and Chablis figured it was too late to hook up with Aaron, so she said, "drop me off at my apartment - 59th and Lexington, right at the IRT. You have been a good boy, so you can come up for some coffee or tea if you want."

You would have thought she had just handed him the keys to Fort Knox. The young kid was all asses and elbows trying to find a parking place. Finally, he squeezed the pickup into a spot so tight Chablis felt like she was getting out of a sardine can.

Chablis used sex to relax, and she had been through some trying days, although two sexual peccadilloes during those days had made things more bearable. Still, she felt all tense, and being with a very young, excited man was titillating her libido. "Why not relax," she said to herself.

PURSUIT

Not once had Chablis ever been turned down for sex by a man because she was transgendered, but she never left anything to surprise, because that was not only deceitful, but might well get you killed if you hooked up with the wrong guy who might be a Bible-thumping maniac of moronic morality. Consequently, she stood beside him and said, "I don't want you to be shocked, so there is something I should tell you. I am a transsexual."

The young man, whom Chablis had not even bothered to ask his name, said, "Mrs. Clinton did not raise no idiot Chablis. Bobby Clinton has been there and done that. I know a real woman when I see one."

Almost laughing, Chablis said, "No, no Bobby. I am a transsexual. OK? You understand."

"Pre or post-op?"

"Pre."

"O.K., I am cool with that but I don't do oral with you then. O.K.?"

"Perfectly O.K., Bobby."

She took him by the hand and led him to the shower. They undressed, showered and Bobby said, "Damn nicest body I have ever seen on a woman, even though you are missing one part."

PURSUIT

"Laughing, Chablis said, "You will never know I don't have it, Bobby. Because what I got and the way I know how to use it will blow your mind."

Suddenly, as they started to embrace, Chablis' land line phone rang, making her realize that her captors must have confiscated her cell as she had forgotten all about it. She grabbed the phone as she gently freed herself from Bobby's grasp. "Hello."

"Where have you been," said a sweet, soft voice.

"Oh Lynton, I will fill you in tomorrow. Right now I am about to get a long love tool in my love canal if you know what I mean, so we will talk in the morning. Call Aaron for me and tell him I will explain everything to you two tomorrow. Right now I have long, hard, tasty business to conduct."

Laughing, Lynton said, "Yeah, O.K. you disgusting whore, you."

Laughing in return, Chablis said, "Yep, and loving every minute of whoredom. You are just jealous!"

She hung up the phone and grabbed Bobby, pulling him lustfully toward her and tilted her head to the left, letting him know she needed a long, passionate, tongue-tapping dance of desire kiss that would rattle their souls.

J. Wayne Frye   183

PURSUIT

Chablis did not make it a habit of having sex with such young men, but she was very attracted to Bobby, who was about 6:2 and very muscular. She felt warm and safe in his masculine arms. She gently pulled him to the bed, and made no effort to tuck in her joy stick that seemed to have no effect on Bobby's intense ardour for her. He lay on top of her and she could feel his huge member pulsating with desire as they passionately kissed. He was young, but had obviously had his share of women as he certainly knew how to make all the right moves. He gently began to work his way down to her perky breasts where he lingered for a few minutes kissing, coddling and sucking with great finesse. Then he started kissing his way toward her stomach where he lingered on her belly button, blowing on it, kissing it and licking it. What came next always frightened Chablis just a bit as she knew some men simply were not able to deal with what was between her legs, despite accepting her as a woman. Bobby, however, was not deterred from his quest for pleasure. He artfully pushed it aside and began to work toward her scrotum. In one smooth motion he placed his hands under her thighs and raised her derriere up to where it was in his face. In order to assist him in his endeavour, she reached down and grabbed her thighs, pulling her legs against her stomach to open up her love hole for him to enjoy. Oh, and enjoy he did. He licked, kissed and sucked delightfully, titillating and tantalizing her desire for that huge tool to park in her garage of lust.

PURSUIT

Slowly, Bobby got on his knees and saw that her hole was quivering with excitement in anticipation of getting the pounding that every gorgeous woman deserves. He would not disappoint, as he guided his member adeptly into the massive opening and started the rhythmic pounding that brought Chablis glorious delight and solidified her grandeur as a woman. She began to moan, and each moan made Bobby pump faster and more furiously as his desire boiled over into a frenzy of carnal delight. He could feel his joy juice building and fighting for release. Suddenly, he thrust long, hard and deep. The pulsating of his member was like a grand symphony to Chablis' body as she worked her sphincter muscle magic, capturing his member in a vice like grip milking and milking every delightful drop of his joy juice.

The evening was spent in glorious rapture as the two were euphorically engaged in a coupling of mind, body and spirit. The next morning, Bobby was so thankful for the evening that Chablis felt overwhelmed that he had enjoyed it so much. For her, it was also a delight, but it was a common occurrence to which she had grown accustomed. It was just part of the glory she felt in being a woman.

Meeting Aaron and Lynton for breakfast, Chablis went over the events of the past two days. After she finished her tale, Lynton gave her a wink and said, "Well, you didn't tell us everything."

PURSUIT

Aaron, knowing what she was hinting about, said, "Lynton, you two can talk that part over in private. I am an old man, and my heart may not be able to take the excitement of one of Chablis' sordid tales of debauchery."

They all laughed and Aaron said, "I am going to visit John Havoc. Don't worry; I will only reveal what is necessary to alert him to what may be an impending terrorist attack. I will see that Don Hart, Manley Martinez and Roy Blount are not mentioned. As for the place in New Jersey where you were taken, it is scrubbed clean by now, so there will be no trace of them. I hate like hell being on the side of the government, but if what you say is correct, many innocents will suffer if we do not thwart this plan to wreck havoc. How is that for a pun – talking to Havoc to prevent havoc?"

They all laughed and Chablis told Lynton, "We shall see Lena now, and find out why she was at the scene of the explosion that day, but first, I must arrange a money transfer to the Hudson sisters. Come; let's pick up my car. I don't feel like riding the subway and the L.I.R.R. to Hempstead. A nice ride to Long Island will be pleasant, and it will give us an opportunity to talk."

Lena was not rich, but her father had left her very comfortable. The death of her two brothers in the useless Iraq War had given her the entire estate as an inheritance. She seemed genuinely thrilled to see Lynton and Chablis. Ushering them into the main sitting room, she offered them tea, which they both graciously accepted. They chatted for awhile until Lena said, "Well, I can tell by your manner Chablis this is not a social call. You are here on business. What is it that you want to know?"

"I will let Lynton explain."

Lynton leaned forward, her brown skin glistening delicately in the morning sunlight that was dancing through the large window to her left. It seemed to almost form a hallo about her dark, silky smooth black hair, which was certainly apropos as she was, indeed, an angel of light in a world that was too often filled with darkness. She very pensively said, "I don't want to be overly inquisitive, but my friends Channa and Ingrid were doing some research on the anarchist attempt ten years ago to assassinate the Prince of Wales, and they found something very interesting. There was a photo that was taken of the dead food cart operator. They recognized you standing nearby. We were all curious as to why you happened to be there that day."

You could see the shock on Lena's face. She licked her bottom lip and took a deep breath as she said, "Really? Oh my, I had forgotten about that."

Chablis chimed in, "Forgotten? How could you forget being near an assassination attempt?"

"Well, well," Lena muttered as she was obviously trying to compose herself and come up with an answer. "You see, I was maybe traumatized and just put it out of my mind all these years."

Smiling, Chablis replied somewhat sarcastically, "Come on Lena. You know me better than that. I am a trained P.I. Level with me; you know that I will eventually find out the truth."

Lena was boxed in and she knew it. Yet, she was reluctant to tell the truth out of fear. She got up and walked over to the window and stared out at the immaculately manicured lawn. Standing there in the rays of the morning sun, she began to sweat. Looking at her, Chablis thought maybe a sexual rendezvous with her might not be bad after all. She had never had sex with a woman, but Lena was certainly appealing. Tall, maybe at least 5:10, with radiant skin that glistened in the sunlight and looked so soft that it would be like touching velvet actually made Chablis tingle a bit thinking about what it would feel like with her. Lena's breasts were large and precisely rounded, and what an ass, its shape rivalled Lynton's in perfection with absolute unparalleled precise symmetry and watching it sway from side to side was a treat for the eyes.

PURSUIT

Seeing Chablis was lost in thought as she eyed Lena, Lynton knew that it was time to rattle Lena's cage. "So, Lena, how about an honest answer? You have had plenty of time to contemplate a lie, but we both know Chablis is a master at uncovering the truth."

Lena and Chablis, both snapping back to reality simultaneously, looked intensely at one another. Chablis was first to speak. "She is right Lena. Whatever secret you harbour, I will find it out. You know that."

Lena took a deep breath and sighed. "O.K, you win, but what I am telling you can cost me my life, Chablis. We are dealing with a government agency that has been known to spirit people to other countries and torture them."

Lynton, without hesitation, said, "The C.I.A."

Walking back to the sofa and taking a seat, Lena replied, "Yes, the C.I.A. You Filipinos should know it well. After all, they are the ones who stirred up the anti-Marcos protestors when he was making moves against corporations. He was a dictator yes, but he was O.K. as long as he was America's dictator, but once he started moving against corporations, that was the end of American support. The C.I.A. is at the root of much evil in the world and in this country. They are supposed to stay out of any activities in the USA, but believe me, ever since they plotted with the mob to assassinate Kennedy, they have been intricately involved in activities aimed at stifling dissent. I know, I know, I sound like a conspiracy nut, but they were involved in Kennedy's demise."

Chablis said, "I don't doubt their involvement at all, but that is ancient history. Right now I need to know their connection to you and to the fact you were at the assassination attempt on the Prince of Wales that day."

"Well, speaking of ancient history, we must go back a long time ago. First, you and most others assumed that the trip on the Suez was about my father's last wish before death from cancer. The only problem was that he was dying from induced cancer. He ingested a poisonous substance which causes cancer. He had inadvertently ingested it when working for the CIA."

Chablis, shocked at the revelation that Lena's father, a known supporter of anarchist ideals, was a C.I.A. operative, shook her to the core. Once again, the sinister intentions if the U.S. government were laid bare. "I can't believe it. So, your father contracted a disease as a result of a poison?"

"Yes, it was developed by a chemical firm in the 1950's in Boston, and used to kill people slowly and make it look like cancer. He was interrogating prisoners in Iraq when a vile that was supposed to be poured into an Iraqi double agent's drink got turned over and he had a cut on his index finger. He absorbed some of it, and that was his end. There is no antidote. So, we were sailing down the Suez as he had always dreamed of it. Just after my father's death, I met Donald Perez, whom you and Chablis knew as a newspaper editor in Manila. Editor he was, but he was also a C.I.A. operative who had assisted them in bringing about the demise of Marcos. He was a young man at the time, and that mistake obligated him to them forever, as the C.I.A. allows you to leave only under one condition – your death. I met him when the C.I.A. sent me on a mission there, and he was my liaison contact. That was also when I met you Lynton, and, of course, your friends Channa and Ingrid."

Chablis, still reeling from the revelations, said, "O.K. so Donald Perez was your C.I.A. contact in the Philippines, which explains that you two might have developed a relationship that led to his leaving you all that money, but the real question here is what you were doing by the food cart that day?"

"I was on a field assignment for the C.I.A."

Chablis instantly knew why she was there. "The C.I.A. knew about the assassination attempt. They knew all about it, and they did nothing."

"Right, Chablis. Their intention was to allow the assassination in order to rouse the public consciousness against the socialist group that was demanding fairness in the country, a redistribution of income from the top to the bottom. What better way than to let someone kill a royal leech that the people think are special and ordained by God to be exalted and worshipped. However, there was also another reason I was there, as when the assassination occurred, I was to take something of great importance in all the confusion. It was something the C.I.A. had been after for many years."

Chablis knew instantly what they were after. "The piece of metal. They knew that Henrietta Hudson had that piece of metal hidden in her food cart, and it was not the anarchists who killed her with an errant explosion but the C.I.A. The C.I.A. had a bomb planted there two. There were people who claimed to have heard two explosions, but that theory was dismissed by the investigators."

Lena's eyes, seemingly on fire, were all Chablis needed to see. She was now telling Lena what happened as her detecting mind was in full mode. "The C.I.A. planted the bomb to kill her at the same time as the assassination, which was cover for you to get the piece of metal. They were more interested in the metal than the Prince of Wales' life, which I can understand, as a rock in the forest is worth more than the life of that royal, arrogant asshole. The C.I.A. and I actually see eye-to-eye on that."

Lynton said, "Hey, the royals know Americans are idiotic celebrity worshipers. Americans are too stupid to understand that a simple thing like calling the President Mr. President is just the same as saying your majesty. I love what the Quebecers do when royalty shows up there. The royals stay out of Quebec, because they know how to treat royalty there. They throw tomatoes at their motorcades."

Lena, smiling now, said, "Yeah, the Canadians may be part of the commonwealth, but those Quebecers don't take lightly to royalty."

They all shared a laugh, but then Chablis got very serious. "What happened? How did you not wind up with the piece of metal?"

"Simple. I panicked in the explosion and was beaten to Henrietta. You know the rest of the story. So, Don Hart winds up with the piece of metal, and I am considered persona non grata for some time, but fortunately, they elected not to eliminate me, but I am always looking over my shoulder to this day."

Chablis got up and walked over to the window. She turned around to face Lena. "I just gave the Hudson sisters around $300,000 as compensation from Don Hart, and guess what? Don Hart did not owe it to them. He did not kill their mother."

Lynton said, "Is it too late to stop the transfer?"

"It is already done. It is instantaneous. Anyway, Don Hart wouldn't care. His father will give him whatever money he needs to escape from the USA."

Lena, in a remorseful tone, said, "I am so sorry. Believe me; I thought Henrietta was the enemy. They said she was in on the assassination plot and had been staking out the area for months and providing the assassin information. All they said was that an assassination would serve as a diversion, and I was to simply go up to the cart, raise the second lid to the left and take out the piece of metal, put it in my purse, go to 63rd and Broadway where I would hand it off to an agent by the mail carrier's storage box. "

Lena, remorsefulness in full bloom within her heart, continued. "Is anything the U.S. government does to maintain the status-quo beyond the realm of possibility? You know what was done in Afghanistan, Iraq and Guantanamo Bay. Hey, my dad was a trained torturer. That nice old man you learned to love in those few days was all façade. He believed anything was permissible in defence of the USA, so he lied about being an anarchist to infiltrate the organization – the elimination of the

PURSUIT

League of Anarchy was his ultimate goal. I was recruited by the agency, though I was leery of their ideology and methods. What could I do? My father was an agent, and my two brothers who were supposed to be fighting in Iraq were actually in Abu Ghraib where they were interrogators, who, no doubt, tortured prisoners. They were not killed in combat as reported, but killed by an Iraqi guard who simply could no longer tolerate watching his countrymen being brutalized in an attempt to get information that most did not even have. Did not Joseph Mengele's family stand by him, despite the atrocities of Auschwitz? I loved my father and brothers, and for that love I sacrificed my principles and my integrity. I am guilty more from not taking a stand against tyranny than from anything I actually did. I know it is not an excuse, but I have served them more out of fear than because of any devotion to a nation that allows unspeakable atrocities to be committed in the name of so-called liberty."

Chablis could mildly understand. Her mother and father listened to the parish priest and ridiculed her because of being transgendered, admonished her for being sinful. Still, she did not show them disrespect, only defiance against the ignorance they showed by relying on someone else to tell them what to think. So, she sympathetically said to Lena, "I can understand Lena that you felt you had to honour your father and brothers, but I cannot excuse it. Even as a

J. Wayne Frye   195

child, I knew that people were wrong when they ridiculed me and pointed the finger of condemnation. You cannot ever let fear keep you from standing against evil and injustice. I believe you are, at heart, a good and decent person. You have cleansed your soul today. Have you not?"

"I have Chablis, and I will stand with you, Lynton and Aaron to fight this evil. Just tell me what I have to do."

Chablis and Lynton were mystified about what would be their next step. Something big was going to happen, and whose side were they on? Should they side with the C.I.A. which has no problem killing innocent people to further its aims of maintaining the status-quo or should they throw in with the anarchists who were only slightly better?

PURSUIT

CHAPTER 9
THE MOST FEARFUL TERROR GROUP

It is well-known by most thinking Americans, which unfortunately are fairly small in number, that they live in a nation filled with slimy little government anti-bodies that go around instilling fear in people so as to more easily control them. Someone afraid is much easier to manipulate than someone who does not see an evil entity lurking around on every street primed to perpetrate chaos. By having children stand with hands over their hearts every morning and pledge allegiance to a flag, the government insures a steady stream of mindless robotons to line up to be cannon fodder in defence of an ideal that does not even exist in reality. Then, of course, there is also the idea promulgated by propagandists that somehow Americans are exceptional, which is also instilled in citizens to assure they never learn the truth about how far the USA is behind the rest of the world when it comes to fairness. Americans work harder, work longer hours, have less vacation time and have fewer social amenities than even most citizens of Third World countries. Yet, mention socialism and the populace reviles at the notion that government should actually help people rather than corporations. How do you overcome the colossal stupidity that manifests itself in people who simply are not smart enough to look for themselves at the rest of the world and see how far behind the USA is?

J. Wayne Frye

PURSUIT

That question was what created a dilemma for Lynton and Chablis. The American people were, in many ways, not worthy of being saved from their own stupidity. However, how do you justify sacrificing people who simply are not smart enough to figure out that they are lining up for their own shackles and chains? Americans were so naive that they actually believed God was on their side. Tell them that the Nazis also believed God was on their side, and they would be incredulous. They simply did not possess the ability to see beyond their own world where they had been so brainwashed with patriotic babble that like Pavlov's dog that salivated when it heard a bell after it was properly conditioned to expect food, Americans snapped to attention and were prepared to die for a lie whenever Old Glory was run up a flagpole or the name of Jesus was invoked. Patriotic ignorance was the chief impediment to Americans ever rising above their own unrecognized mediocrity.

Chablis asked Lena if the C.I.A. was planning to set idly by and allow a terrorist attack in order to stir up the populace. She was not sure, but she indicated that it was way past time for another motivational attack to solidify the population in concert to a cause that would rouse its patriotic fervour.

Chablis looked at Lena and said, "You with us or against us?"

PURSUIT

"I am scared as hell, but I am with you. I am sick of always siding with the oppressors. What do you want of me?"

"We want you to simply act as nothing has happened," said a determined Chablis. "Right now, I know something big is planned by the anarchist element, but the C.I.A. is a bigger threat than they are, because they are, no doubt, going to aid and abet the destruction for their own personal aims. They obviously have a mole in the anarchist group, and I also am sure the group has me targeted for elimination. I think it best that both you and Lynton stay clear of me, because you two are not targets yet, but the C.I.A. will eliminate anyone that gets in its way. They have already proved what they are capable of at Guantanamo. To them, torture is just another in the long list of justifiable means to protect the freedom that we don't really have. They are a much bigger threat to democracy than any terrorists who are lurking about."

Lena very gently placed her right hand on Chablis' left leg. "I am with you." Then she got a coy smile as she continued, "But just in case I meet my end, I'd sure love that sexual rendezvous with you before I go."

They both laughed heartedly, as did Lynton, who said, "Maybe I had better go and leave your two alone."

PURSUIT

Again, they all laughed and Lena chimed in, directing her comment toward Lynton. "I have been after her for years, and one of these days she is going to give me what I want out of sympathy if nothing else."

Chablis offered a slightly different take on things. "Hey, I am after demons of deceit, not sensual serpents of desire, girl."

Lynton said, "I am the one glorified by Wayne Frye as a demon fighter. Let's put our heads together for the good of humanity. The C.I.A. operatives are demons, and I have faced some of the toughest demons imaginable. Let's take these guys on."

Chablis and Lena nodded their heads in agreement and a bond of determination was formed. All hell was about to break lose.

When Hell Waits Patiently

How many drops must gather to the skies
Before the cloud-burst comes, we may not know;
How hot the fires ill under hells must glow
Ere the volcano's scalding lavas rise,
Can none say; but all but the hour is sure!
Who dreams of vengeance has but to endure
He may not say how many blows must fall,
How many lives be broken on the wheel,
How many corpses stiffen beneath the pall,

J. Wayne Frye 200

PURSUIT

How many martyrs fix the blood-red seal;
But certain is the harvest time of hate!
And when weak moans by an indignant world
Echoed to an arrogant throne are hurled,
Who listens and hears the mutterings of Fate!
Ah, at the door is hell unbowed and unfurled!
Anarchy is in the revolution many may say,
But perhaps it was anarchy that was felled,
For that which was, may in judgment lay.

Aaron Adams was with John Havoc, informing him that an avalanche of evil was about to be unleashed on an unsuspecting populace by two opposing forces. As they were talking, the three C.I.A. agents who had been in the alley that night walked in with the Police Commissioner.

What is it that gives people in positions of power a sense of elevated importance? Truth be told, most people do not rise to the top on merit, but rather as a result of connections and how much ass they kiss on the way up. Pearson Adelson was one of those pompous, arrogant, over-educated assholes whose father had been a precinct captain who greased the skids for his son, getting him promoted when much more competent individuals were passed over. That is the way of the world; nepotism makes it possible for those with the right parents to get ahead whether it is in Hollywood or the police department. Who you know and who your parents are means much more than any talent you might have.

J. Wayne Frye   201

PURSUIT

Adelson had many run-ins with Aaron over the years, so there was animosity between the two, but Adelson took no time in letting the feds know he was a man of action. He barked at Aaron, "Take a hike peeper."

Aaron, who never cowered in fear before anyone, replied, "I'll take a hike up your ass Adelson if you fuck with me."

"Peeper, you're out of your league, here. I told you to get out of here."

Aaron, taking exception to being called peeper, said, "Hey Adelson, maybe your right. I am a peeper. I peeped at that fat wife of yours last week and puked."

Then Aaron started to walk away and looking directly at Adelson, said, "These C.I.A. torturers might like to know where the League of Anarchists camp was over in Jersey, but a low-life peeper like me is of no interest to them I am sure. They'll get a lot more out of a high class ass-kissing, nepotistic jerk like you, because you are so fucking smart you have your finger on the pulse of the city. That's why the crime rate is so goddamn low, I suppose."

One of the feds said, "Wait Adams, we're looking for your partner Chablis Chavez, and we'd love to know about the league's camp."

PURSUIT

Taken aback, Adleson just stood there dumbfounded. Aaron let a snarl curl across his lower lip. "O.K., I can help you with the Jersey camp, but they have all skedaddled. It is in the marshlands on Coleman Road near the Teterboro airport. But you know what; you already know that, because you have a mole in the camp. What you really want is Chavez. And guess what? No amount of torture will make me give her up, even if I knew where she was. Anyway, she is only contacting me when she wants, as she knows you will be shadowing her. You boys are afraid of something, and what you better be afraid of his me and Chavez. You fuck with us and you'll all be pushing up daisies. We don't go down easy."

John Havoc had stood there through it all, enjoying Aaron's disrespectful attitude toward assholes. He smiled at Adelson and said, "So, can the peeper go now, sir?"

Adelson looked at the head fed who nodded in the affirmative. Aaron, really smiling now, said to Adelson, "I take it back. Your wife's not that fat, but her damn asshole is as wide as the Grand Canyon from all the cocks she takes up it."

Adelson broke immediately toward Aaron who pivoted right, jerking his head back to avoid the right cross he delivered. Aaron just grabbed him around the waist and shoved him toward the feds as he said, "You guys deserve each other."

J. Wayne Frye

PURSUIT

John Havoc smiled and gave Aaron a knowing nod. The fed got on his cell-phone, and, no doubt thought Aaron, was telling someone out front to tail him.

Sure as rain on a hot, humid overcast day, the tail was there, but Aaron decided not to shake him. At this point, it didn't really matter. The Anarchist League had a clandestine back-up place to hide, and it was there that their detailed final plans for a grand and glorious assault on the city were being hatched.

When Chablis called to see if Sherry and Pamela Hudson had received their financial windfall, they were effusive with thanks. However, Chablis was specific in saying that it was not she they should thank, but Don Hart who had lived with the thought of what he had done for years, but that the truth was the C.I.A. was responsible for their mother's death, but that he still wanted them to have the money. Chablis asked if they would be willing to talk to the *New York Times,* and they enthusiastically agreed. It would be up to Chablis to arrange the time, and she would do that as soon as she took care of some unfinished business.

The mole in the League was well-positioned to make certain that the organization did maximum damage to rally a now somewhat complacent populace to once again support another lie like Iraq was. The C.I.A. was poised to fool the

PURSUIT

American public into believing a foreign power was behind the coming anarchist attack. It was not hard to fool the American people. Many still believed after so many years that Iraq had something to do with 9/11. If they wanted to go after the conspirators, they should have insisted on the invasion of Saudi Arabia from where the hijackers hailed, but that would never happen as the Saudis had too much pull with the Bush family and Cheney's old firm Halliburton had too many contracts with them.

As Hitler said, tell a lie often enough and people will begin to believe it. The American people simply were too dumb to look for the truth. Too many of them relied on the lies promulgated by FOX NEWS. It was so much easier to sit on the sofa and watch the ballgame while others did your thinking for you.

In the League's new compound, preparations were being made for war on American greed, but within the ranks were those who saw it as an opportunity for destruction rather than an opportunity to build a better society. Far too many of the conspirators had not embraced the ideology of hope for a better tomorrow, but rather had decided that the destruction of the old order was a way for them to act out deep rooted anger that had piled up over the years. They were now looking for revenge not redemption. This was simply playing into the hands of the real conspirators, and in the end, the government that represented the few would again have the populace under its control as people would fall into line to stand against what they would see as an attempt to bring the grand American democracy to its knees. The truth was democracy had been on its knees for years, ever since Reagan had decided any act to combat communism was sanctified. The U.S.A. had won the war against communism as greed had triumphed, but the populace had to always be kept fearful of some entity that was out there to undermine the freedom Americans believed they had. In the 1950's, 60's, 70's and 80's it was the Godless communists and then along came the Islamic terrorists who wanted to make the world bow before Mohammad rather than Jesus. Oh, that really angered Americans, because they loved Jesus even more than their country.

Remember that the anarchists had a weapon that the C.I.A. desperately wanted, but they did not want to confiscate it until the last minute, as they wanted the League to believe in its invincibility. They would be allowed to use the weapon under strict observance by the mole. Once enough damage had been done to congeal the people into a unified force willing to once again sacrifice freedom to protect freedom, then the weapon would be secured for the proper authorities to control it, and the USA would have a weapon that would allow it to make the world cower in fear before its might.

PURSUIT

The mole was desperate to communicate with the C.I.A., but a security lockdown had made everyone suspect and as they prepared for the coming calamity, each person had an observer to watch over him or her to assure no breach of security endangered the mission. Down in the depths of the new camp, a rumble could be heard, and in a few seconds the whirring low hum of the piece of metal was seemingly sanctifying what was about to occur. The three beacons were taken by Bob Swift, Lou Swartz and Bruno. The humming metal was picked up by Justin, and thus the stage was set for the supreme act of revolution. Only among the four was the C.I.A. mole who had other ideas that were formulating in his head, as he had to notify his handlers of the coming carnage, which was going to be far more vast than had been imagined.

To understand the plans one must first comprehend the vastness of them, as never before had such a stupendous act of terror even been contemplated. The four men strode out into an open field where they all got into a van and headed for Manhattan.

It was becoming dark when the pine forests and sand wastes of the New Jersey marshlands gave way to the beginning of urban New York City. Rolling across the George Washington Bridge the riders were all sullen and silent, each contemplating what was going to be done. A dark cloud cover hung over the bridge wrought of mists driven from the upper regions by the chills that hurried after the setting sun. The wind blew in gusts and preyed vampire-like on the individual energies of the anarchists. Clouds were rising smoke-like from the river rim and mingling with the flatter masses seeming to engulf everything in a foreboding darkness. The silence was finally broken by Lou Swartz, who was still reeling from the fact that Don Hart had deserted the project. He, in a soft whisper said, "Violent diseases often demand violent remedies, and this nation has been suffering from the disease of greed for far too long. The surgeon must be gentle at heart, but he spares not the gangrenous limb. We are going to cut off a mighty limb."

The truth was that Lou and his friend Bruno, had long ago given up on changing anything, as they both had decided that America was not worth saving. For that reason, they assumed that revolution was simply no longer possible in a nation that had been so completely sacrificed at the altar of greed. In the end, only its total destruction would lead to a world free of a nation that used intimidation and wealth to make greed an epidemic that infected all of mankind. Even China, a nation still called communist by the United States had humbly bowed to the evil of greed and it had, like the USA, embraced and sanctified a gulf between the haves and have-nots as the cost for a world where money was the ultimate goal of all, for money was the true God of the world now. Yes, money and its worship had conquered all. Even religion, with its constant hand out was afflicted with greed.

Lou and Bob both lamented the desertion of Don Hart, but it was to be expected. After all, Don's father, Robert Hernandez, was a man of wealth, and in the end, wealth always wins out. However, this time Lou, Bob and Bruno would see that wealth did not win, because this time the destruction would be so devastating that a city would lay in such ruin nothing, no amount of money, could resurrect it.

As Lou, Bob and Bruno thought of the coming destruction, Justin, an old man who had decided that prison life was too much to bear and, thereby, made a call to the government offering to give up all his anarchist friends for freedom, as the C.I.A. mole, was trying to figure how he would contact the agency to alert them to what was about to occur. The situation was tenuous, and he fretted that he might not be able to contact them in time. He desperately wanted to live, because he had given up a lifetime of devotion to a cause in order to live out his life free of prison bars with a tidy income to make him comfortable in his old age. He had alerted the agency about Chablis that very night at the banquet when he had so aptly played his role as an old anarchist. He was rather proud of that performance.

PURSUIT

As these four were rolling across the GW Bridge, Chablis, Lynton, Channa and Ingrid were all sleeping, but dancing in their minds were thoughts of how they might ward off the coming calamity. They all knew that in the U.S the government had a long list of terrorist organizations, but the truth be known, the number one terrorist group was not some entity of fear lurking about in the shadows, but rather, the most fearful terror group of all was the U.S. government itself.

CHAPTER 10
ONLY PROBLEM IS WHICH ONE

In the nondescript office building located at 1111 Lexington Avenue, the sign on the front read Melton Investments. Yes, it was an investment company, but it invested in deception, subterfuge, torture and the overthrow of legitimately elected governments all over the world. This was a front company for the C.I.A., and that day there was a flurry of activity as the agents there were anxiously awaiting word on the impending terrorist attack from the mole that had infiltrated the League of Anarchy.

As the Melton offices buzzed with activity, Chablis was just arising from slumber and her phone rang. A voice from afar said, "You must stop the destruction Chablis. The C.I.A. is out of control, and they are about to allow destruction as you have never seen before."

Chablis, not recognizing the voice, said, "Who is this?"

"This is the *Spirit of Che Guevara*, resurrected from the grave," was the reply.

"Oh my. Oh my. Where are you Rodrigo? You have been gone for so long. I thought you dead."

"Many will die, if you do not stop it."

J. Wayne Frye   211

PURSUIT

Excited that she was hearing from the man she had fallen in love with in her famous case, documented by Wayne Frye in the best seller, *Chablis and the Terrorist Who Resurrected the Spirit of Che Guevara*, Chablis was overwhelmed with emotion, but the voice had no time for emotion, as it continued, "Be aware that the real danger is in the C.I.A. which is determined to bring about chaos to effectuate a dictatorship of sorts by scaring the people into complacent acceptance of government tyranny to, as that buffoon of banality, George Bush said, root out the terrorists. The terrorists are not hiding in a cave in some Third World country. The terrorists are hiding in plain sight in government buildings. The terrorists are the very people who are supposed to be protecting the populace from terrorists. The fate of the city and of the nation is in your hands, Chablis. Look around and you will see what must be done. The real lair of evil is in the Melton Investment Building on Lexington Avenue right near you. Do something now, as time is rapidly running out for the innocents who are about to be sacrificed for the evil intentions of a government that no longer represents or cares for the people."

The phone went dead and the silence was almost deafening. Chablis sat on the side of her bed contemplating what to do. She knew that the *Spirit of Che* had once saved the people from a similar tyranny.

PURSUIT

Their voice from afar rattled her soul. It was as if it came from another era, another place that had been drifting in the sands of time. It had great power that would lead her to walk in the shadow of the valley of death but fear no evil, for she was with the warrior, Aaron Adams, who slew tyrants. She also had the slayer of demons by her side now. Yes, Lynton Viñas, demon-fighter, would be her strong right arm in this battle.

She would stand up to the murder and evil that was hidden behind the mask of tyranny represented by the U.S. government. The killers of hope she had seen in the alley that night, three C.I.A. agents who were pit bulls of evil ready to devour the good and innocent. They were all fat with arrogance and self-righteous disregard for justice. They were going to chew on human hearts and under the cloak of government hide their crimes. The evil within them was the most insidious imaginable, because they were presented to the world as loyal, devoted guardians of good.

To these evil minions of hate, children were but pawns to be sacrificed, their brains scattered on the streets in homage to greed and the protection of the wealthy. They cloaked themselves in the light of patriotism but in the shadows that surrounded them the evil of hypocrisy hid from the genuine light of hope. There's was a ghastly masquerade that disguised evil in the cloak of patriotism. They all rode white horses, but beneath

J. Wayne Frye   213

the bridles was the blood of innocents as they were the four horsemen of the apocalypse bringing doom and destruction. People believed they rode against evil, but the truth was the horsemen themselves were the real evil. They all wore the kingly crowns that signified the mark of the beast, the beast of self-righteous arrogance and greed. These horsemen were kings of deceit above all law who destroyed hope under the galloping hoofs of hatred and despair.

The early part of the day was spent with Lynton, Channa, Ingrid and Aaron all formulating plans to immediately find out where the terrorist attack was to take place and somehow get the League of Anarchy to curtail their plans by letting them know that the C.I.A. was setting them up. Yet, how did they do it?

Also, how did they protect the three conspirators who had left the anarchist group? They had to see that they got to safety free of the vindictive government that cared not if you had a change of heart, because once a terrorist in the minds of the righteous, who ruled with complete impunity, always a terrorist. In America there simply were no second chances. Well, unless you were rich or part of the privileged class, then there were unlimited chances.

The night before, Chablis had patiently waited for a call from Don Hart, but none came. She had already placed the ad in the paper as promised for that day. Still, though worried about Don and his colleagues, her real concern was just where were Justin, Lou, Bruno and Bob? They were about to unleash hell on New York City, and time was running short.

Lynton sent her two charges, Channa and Ingrid, off to the library again to try and ferret out anything unusual that was happening the next few days in the city. Finding an even innocuous event might be a clue to where the conspirators would strike.

Aaron, Lynton and Chablis were ready to tackle the C.I.A. head on at Melton Investments. On the way there, Chablis whispered to Lynton, "Don't be surprised at what you hear come out of Aaron's mouth. He is not very respectful of authority."

Lynton, a half smile pursing her lips, said, "Oh yeah, like you are so respectful of authority."

With a pace both stately and fast, over land beneath their feet which they had so often trod, Aaron and Chablis, with Lynton in tow, were trampling across the streets which had for years been home to them and those they protected. In reality, they were a mighty troop of good that shook the ground with dignity and devotion to justice in a land where it was always in short supply.

PURSUIT

Anyone looking at the three as they made their way down Lexington Avenue would have thought they were about to witness an old fashioned shootout in a dusty western street. The strides were true and sure with a confident air as they appeared to be intoxicated with verve and devotion to the cause of justice. They were Wyatt Earp, Virgil Earp and Doc Holliday about to walk into the O.K. Corral.

Crossing 12th Avenue, the light blinking go-go-go in bright green, they were three warriors swift and free come to stand against the tyrants of tyranny. The building was on their left and the three boldly walked in through the revolving door without any hesitation. The three guards behind the reception desk looked with trepidation at the three who stood before them defiant and unafraid. Aaron said, "Get the head asshole out here now. We have something important to discuss."

Though not panic stricken, one guard placed his hand inside his coat pocket, obviously to fondle his gun and get ready for any eventuality. Aaron said calmly, "Pull it out asshole and a lot of people will die; you being the very first one."

He hit the buzzer as two other guys in high-priced black suits walked over. Aaron smiled at them and said to Lynton and Chablis "Girls, these guys are asking for some trouble. Wait outside for me."

PURSUIT

Chablis shook her head empathically no, turned to Lynton and said, "You go. You aren't packing."

Lynton looked down at her heels, moved close to the guy on her left and said, "My heels are more deadly than a gun. I can have my heels grinding his crotch before he has his gun drawn." Then something surprising came out of the mouth of demure little Lynton that shocked Aaron and Chablis. Smiling directly at the guy, she continued, "He'll spend the rest of the day picking up what is left of his balls off the floor."

Aaron and Chablis both laughed out loud as they had never heard anything like that uttered by the demure, dainty, prim and proper Lynton. Aaron, looking at Lynton, said, "Well put little lady."

The first guy out the elevator was immediately recognized by Chablis and Aaron as the guy from the alley that night. He acted as if he were clothed in blood and flame, a hired God to rain down terror on all who dared question his authority. They, of course, looked at him as nothing more than a hired thug whose primary job was to protect the privileged class.

The two guys behind him were brazen, cocky and bold in their manner, standing there in their expensive suits as if they were some exalted mighty warriors with a grand and glorious mission. The head guy, arrogantly, without any trepidation, said to Aaron, "Not a good idea to come here and make threats Adams. I know why you are here, and frankly, we don't give a damn about you and your bitch here anymore. So, take a hike, before you get trouble you can't handle."

Aaron, cold and deliberate, replied, "I don't make threats. I simply state facts. There are three of you behind the desk, two of you in front of the desk, and now the three facing me. You know I carry a big bastard of a 45, so I only have six shots, but there will be six of you dead before I hit the ground. I am not the guy you want to fuck with, believe me. You are standing here like royalty, expecting me to scrape and bow because I am supposed to be scared of people who represent the government. I pay your salaries assholes. You are here to serve me, not the other way around."

"Look Adams, whatever you think you know makes no difference. You are a voice crying in the wilderness. The public believes the government, because they look to us for protection from the evil entities that are trying to destroy our freedom."

"Bullshit," shouted Aaron "to patriotic babble the poor dumb slobs may bow, but I can see through the deceit and manipulation. I am looking at the only real danger to freedom right here and right now. We are here to let you know that we know all about what you plan to do, and I have an incredibly big mouth and a friend at the *New York Times* who likes to listen to whatever I have to say."

Moving slightly toward Aaron the head honcho said, "Be very careful, very careful. Graveyards are full of assholes like you who thought they were going to tackle the C.I.A. and come out on top. I'll put on your headstone *here lies another poor slob who thought he could take on the U.S. government.*"

"Won't happen buddy, dead men don't have head stones carved. I'll carve one: *here lies an asshole who tried to tangle with Aaron Adams.*"

The guy to the left of Lynton made a big mistake. He started a movement that indicated he was going to pull his gun, and without hesitation, she, the demure little Lynton, lifted her incredibly muscular dancer's perfectly shaped left leg and extended her spiked high heel right to his crotch and with perfect balance, the former professional toe tapper stood there sternly erect as the guy quivered in fear and gently removed his hand from inside his pocket as he said, "I'm cool baby. I'm cool."

"Damn right you're cool – better be big guy," Chablis said smiling. "You my fine feathered friend are in the company of the dynamic dynamo."

PURSUIT

The head man said, "Be cool guys. Keep 'um holstered. We don't want the sound of gunfire causing civilians to rush in here."

Aaron leaned in a little closer to the guy and almost whispered. "One request and we'll go in peace. Tell your mole to call it off, because some nosy P.I. has uncovered the plot. Anarchy and government subterfuge that way can both bow and grin to common sense just for today and save lives as well as millions of taxpayer dollars. What you say?"

"You win Adams. Would love to call it all off. Only problem is we have lost contact with the mole. For all we know, one of you might have bumped him."

"We haven't bumped anyone, yet, but it is still early. I suggest you find the mole and do it in a hurry. If we find him, we'll have him call you for confirmation. Your name?

"No name, just tell him Agent 88 can confirm."

"The mole's name?"

"Justin Hartman. And if you get him killed, you will be in some big trouble."

Chablis and Lynton were shocked that Justin, the man who seemed such a dedicated anarchist, was the mole. They looked at one another in disbelief.

Aaron said, "We'll be in touch 88."

The agent very carefully, holding up his right hand, reached inside his breast pocket with his left and brought out a business card. "You can reach me here," then he looked over at the guard by the switchboard and continued, "He'll connect you no matter where I am."

Aaron looked at the card and it read *Brent L. Easton, Vice-President of Marketing*. Aaron gave him the smile with lots of teeth showing and said, "Yeah, Vice President of marketing bull-shit to the manipulated masses." Then he signalled for the two girls to start backing out of the building. They very carefully moved toward the door. The shootout at O.K. Corral had been avoided, temporarily at least, and the guy who had Lynton's heels in his balls felt like he had just been saved from a fate worse than death.

When they hit the street, Chablis giggled as she said to Aaron, "Looks like little Lynton is more than just a demon fighter. She might be ready to take on the arrogant authorities of mayhem, and see what real demons are like. She will find out fighting the devil is much easier than fighting city hall, the NYPD, the C.I.A. and the F.B.I. Now those places harbour some real demons."

PURSUIT

Aaron glanced over his shoulder and said, "You got that right, Chablis. We got a tail, three of 'um. Let's split up and give them the shakes. Hit the streets and find those anarchists."

"O.K., we'll head over to the library and see what Channa and Ingrid found out. Later."

As the girls were walking up Lexington Avenue, they had no idea that in a subway tunnel nearby in an abandoned boiler room the conspirators were meticulously planning their attack. These were people who knew palaces existed on the street above while others wallowed in poverty, and they were about to strike a blow for those who had been confined to restaurants, hotels and retail stores working for $12 an hour to serve people who made $12 a second. They were going to bring down the kings so bold who held golden staffs while wearing gold woven robes. These knights in the tunnel were serving revenge on the those who sat at the table of plenty, but they had forgotten the humanity that had to go along with revolution, for they were about to destroy the very people whom they wanted to save in the process of bringing down the high and mighty. Bruno and Lou were like two inmates just released from the asylum waiting to wreck havoc on a world they blamed for all their ills. Bob Swift had long ago lost touch with reality as his hatred for humanity now exceeded his compassion for those he once longed to help. Like Bruno and Lou, his mission was now more about revenge than redemption. Then there was the fly in the ointment, the mole in the hole, the Judas Iscariot in their midst, ready to betray his colleagues with a kiss on the cheek in repayment to the Pharisees for freeing him."

These men all had forgotten the reason for revolution. It was the maids in three million dollar condos who had to go home to a hovel in Spanish Harlem, the person asking if you wanted French Fries with your hamburger, the man sweeping up streets in old sneakers while the rich walked past in Bruno Magli shoes, it was all the little people who made the well-oiled machinery of capitalism hum so the rich could dine on caviar while the masses begged for a bowl of rice. These were the people who had waited for so long on cloudy days for a bit of sunshine while they fumbled and begged with palsied hands. These were the people who deserved to be lifted from despair, but these conspirators were about to dispatch them with those who caused their misery. Now, the conspirators were preparing to make these people pay the price for greed along with the rich.

Meeting Channa and Ingrid at the midtown library, Chablis was surprised when they handed her a long list of events that were taking place over the next week in the city. They all had a seat at a large table as Chablis meticulously scanned the list, her penchant for finding the most miniscule detail making her wave off the question

PURSUIT

Ingrid was about to ask. Chablis was in full concentration mode. Lynton put her right index finger to her lips to indicate complete silence so Chablis could concentrate. Each item on the list held Chablis' attention for a few seconds as she thought over the possibilities.

Misery was there staring her in the face. Child after child would face doom with the dust of death piled high by those who had lost sight of the real reason for revolution. Into misery had the children of the poor been brought to the world as the religious paragons of virtue had insisted they not be aborted. It was a sin to abort a child, but no sin to allow it to live in poverty. That was the kind of convoluted thinking that kept the cycle of poverty continuing so that the rich would always have a steady stream of workers' to exploit. Murder, fraud and anarchy were at the heart of a system that was based on exploitation. The poor might as well lie in the street and let the wheels of capitalism grind them into oblivion. Chablis' mind was racing now, thinking of the exploited, thinking of how she might avoid catastrophe planned by both the government and the anarchists. Something had to be there, something was perfect for the use of that new weapon the anarchists possessed.

Chablis eased back in her chair and stared at the far wall in frustration. Again Ingrid started to say something, but Lynton immediately shook her

J. Wayne Frye   224

head from side to side, making sure Chablis' concentration was not interrupted.

Looking at the far wall right in front of her, an image started to form of her two groups of foes. A light mist of an image arose in her mind, small at first, weak and frail like a vapour penetrating a thick heavy veil.

Staring, staring, staring, the clouds and mist began to lift in her mind. There was a kaleidoscope of thought striding fast now and it was as if lightning was about to flash and the roar of thunder would soon rumble from the sky. The clouds opened up and the brightness softened the clash of lightning and thunder as the great scale of hope was beginning to balance. In the far distance was the dawn of hope as plumes of rain fell gently from a cloudless sky, but alas, it was not rain but the crimson dew of revelation. Halleluiah, the answer was so easy that no one would ever suspect it. The answer was there for any inquiring mind to easily figure out.

Again, Ingrid was about to say something, but Chablis said, "Hush, hush. I am going to lay it all out for you. It is as easy as one, two, three. Where is the biggest congregation of people going to be when the baseball season opens tomorrow?

Lynton chimed in, "We're Filipina. We don't know anything about baseball."

J. Wayne Frye   225

PURSUIT

"Right, right, of course you would not know." She pointed at the far wall where a huge poster hung between two pillars announcing the Yankee baseball season opener tomorrow afternoon and in attendance would be the mayor and the governor, and yes the pièce de résistance, the only reasonable target for maximum effect, the President of the USA.

"Oh my," said Ingrid as she got up and said, "I have to ask now. Can't wait. I need to use the washroom."

They all laughed, as Chablis said, "Please do."

Lynton asked, "What do we do?"

Chablis was contemplative again. "Hey, there are a bevy of people who are not needed. All those government officials are nothing but a drain on the taxpayers, but they always say that you eliminate an incompetent official, there is always another incompetent person waiting to take his place. Besides there will be a lot of average Joe's there, too - idiots who saved up money so they could watch a bunch of millionaires pumped up on steroids do one of the most useless things ever invented, hit a ball with a round bat. Hey, that is one of society's most valuable human beings, a man who can hit a round ball 400 feet. Now, we all know that is much more important than teaching a kid how to add, subtract, spell, etc. or doing social work in the ghetto. Society really has its priorities in order rewarding those buffoons with a bat."

Lynton chimed in, "Never seen a game, and from what you describe, I never want to see one. However, I have a feeling that you are planning on being at this game. So, are we alerting the authorities about what you have deduced?"

"You can be assured the C.I.A. already knows. The C.I.A. exists to keep Americans in fear. The current President is no friend of the C.I.A. and the Republican Congress deplores him because he has not been a profound promoter of war. Although he wound up being more a moderate Republican than a real Democrat, the power structure sees him as a small impediment to corporate dominance and a huge impediment to more overt interference in the affairs of other nations. The Republicans love sending the poor to die for the weapons manufacturers. The chicken hawks who never served in the military think the poor are nothing but cannon fodder for the machine of capitalism. My guess is the C.I.A., in collusion with Republican party leaders, is about to sit idly by while the President is assassinated, and since the governor and mayor are both Democrats, they see no need to save them either. I am sure that if they could, they would have the Vice-President at the game, too, and then the next in line is the Speaker of the House of Representatives, a Republican.

PURSUIT

This is a nation that never had a coup d'état, but the C.I.A. is capable of almost anything. The military leaders actually came close in 1966, but Lyndon Johnson was too smart for them."

Chablis, just as Ingrid returned, said, "Channa, Ingrid look in the balcony near the rare book section. You see there two men in suits who genuinely look out of place. Go up there and do something, anything to get their attention away from me and Lynton. We need to be free of a tail right now."

Ingrid said, "How do you know they are tailing you?"

Lynton interjected, "Believe me, she knows. Do as she asks."

Channa got up, took Ingrid by the hand and said, "Come on girl. You love vamping men, let's see some action."

Ingrid offered her astute observation. "If they are men, then they are vulnerable to my irresistible allure."

Chablis said, "We'll be in touch. Go back to the hotel afterward."

Ingrid feeling a bit adventuresome said, "Can we take them with us?"

Lynton said, "Not a good idea, girl. Curtail your libido. Anyway, I hear C.I.A. men are not great in the lovemaking department."

Chablis offered her opinion. "Believe me; you will be happier with the bellboy than those assholes."

Ingrid, always giddy with quips, said, "Um', bellboy uh? Maybe I will ask for some room service, and I mean some real good old fashioned get it on room service."

Channa, always prim and proper, said as she was now tugging on Ingrid, "Move it girl and stop thinking about men. The world is about to come down around us and you are thinking about sex."

Still wanting to engage in frivolity, as she walked away with Channa, Ingrid said, "If the world is coming down around me I want to be in bed with a virile lover just in case it is my last time."

Chablis looked at Lynton and said, "That girl likes men almost as much as I do."

Lynton replied, "More."

They laughed and waited for Channa and Ingrid to work their sensuous magic. It would not take long.

PURSUIT

One would think that professionals are individuals who never would let anything come between them and the appointed job they are assigned, but with two magnificent specimens of womanhood like Channa and Ingrid offering the distraction, all bets were off. As they climbed the spiral staircase to the rare book section, one of the operatives kept an eye on Lynton and Chablis while the other observed Ingrid and Channa. Oh my, what a pleasure it was to observe them.

Ingrid, ascended the stairs very slowly, making sure each stretch of her luscious limb exposed a maximum of long, lithe, delightfully soft brown leg that seemed to be begging for the touch of a lover. This was a woman who was as ripe as a dew covered watermelon waiting to be harvested. Each sensual breath she took made her breasts rise and fall like a magnificent sailing ship floating gracefully over undulating waves on an azure sea of desire. A seductive smile crept across her lips as she gracefully moved toward the agent who by now was so captivated that the bulge in his pants signified desire had overtaken the caution that was supposed to be exercised when on duty. Ingrid was dynamite in a dress and she was lighting a fuse that sizzled slowly and surely before she exploded with sexual prowess that was the stuff of legends. Looking at her soft lips made the agent fantasize about them being wrapped around that thing which was bulging in his pants. His breathing quickened and beads of perspiration began to form on his brow. His erection had become so uncomfortable that he had to reach down and adjust it. Ingrid had done her job magnificently as the distraction had worked to perfection.

Channa, on the other hand, always wore longer dresses which did not expose as much leg, but her hips swayed methodically from side to side, making a man's mind instinctively imagine what was under that tight-fitting garment that sensuously hugged every curve. This was a woman who was long and tall and had it all. As the old saying goes, she was hotter than the steam coming out the locomotive called the Wabash Cannonball.

The other agent took his eyes off Lynton and Chablis for a second to admire Channa's curves and in a blink of the eye Lynton and Chablis were up and out the entrance, down the steps and into a cab. By the time the two agents had recovered their composure and rushed out of the library, Chablis and Lynton were long gone. They stood there on the steps bewildered as Channa and Ingrid gracefully and alluringly strolled by them. Ingrid gave them a smile, winked and seductively licked her lips. Damn, how she loved tantalizing men.

"So," asked Lynton as Chablis was calling Aaron, "what do we do now?"

PURSUIT

"Just a minute," said Chablis as she talked to Aaron, telling him she had deduced the calamity was planned for Yankee Stadium. She hung up, turned to Lynton and said, "Aaron says we need not contact the C.I.A., as they are never going to change things because of our revelation. This is not about the anarchist group as much as it is about eliminating a President they see as an impediment to what they want."

"So, what is out next move," asked Lynton.

"Your guess is as good as mine."

Then, an idea popped into Chablis' head. She said, "Mac McAlister! Oh my, there are two moles. Mac McAlister and Justin Hartman are both moles. The reason Mac McAlister was with me from the very beginning was because he knew I had a connection to Lena Langley because of the inheritance." Then she laughed and continued. "He was fucking me for the C.I.A, trying to find out how much I knew. Damn, I will have to send the C.I.A. a note of thanks. That was some good stuff."

"Wait a minute," said an inquisitive Lynton. "I don't know Mac McAllister."

"He was at the facility where they imprisoned me. He and I had three trysts that I thought were serious lovemaking sessions, but they were nothing but forays by a C.I.A. agent to see how much I knew about tellurium. Fact is, I had never even heard of it at the time. He never mentioned it, but now, looking back, he was very inquisitive about my relationship with Lena. Yeah, Mac is a mole, too. So, there is Justin and Mac, two moles who apparently are so deep underground right now that they can't get word to the C.I.A. about the attack. They might not even be aware that the other one is a mole. In this country there are sometimes more informants than miscreants."

"That is the key, underground. Roy said something to me while we were having sex in my cell. He said, 'I am going to plunge so far up your ass that it will be deeper than a subway tunnel used for a hideout from the law.' That is it; the plotters are hiding in a subway tunnel. Only problem is which one?"

PURSUIT

CHAPTER 11
FIGHT FOR THE SOUL OF A NATION

With steps as violent as a raging storm,
Over the heads of men of ill-intent,
Two strong-willed women were there,
And their rising rage was floating in the air.

As flowers beneath their footsteps waken,
As stars from night's loose hair are shaken,
As waves arise when loud winds brazenly call,
Fear springs forth from where their steps fall.

Ah, the multitudes of the teaming city
Were about to be ankle deep in blood.
But from the hearts of two maidens often serene
Was dedication to justice bold and keen.

True anarchy from the government given birth,
Fairness laid dead earth upon earth.
Hope fled with hoofs that did people grind,
Leaving misery and despair behind.

A rushing light of clouds and splendour,
A sense, awakening and yet tender,
Was heard and felt at day's coming close
As these words of joy and fear arose.

"Though we are but two souls in flight,
We are indignant with rage ready to fight.
We stand against tyranny to never flee,
We are dynamic Lynton and mighty Chablis."

J. Wayne Frye

PURSUIT

The test of human worth is the power to minister human happiness to the masses that thirst for justice. By that standard, American civilization has proved a colossal failure. Sanctimonious politicians, pompous tycoons and pontificating preachers talk of embracing hope, but nothing of depth through long and weary centuries has been accomplished but the piling up of more riches by the few and the rewards for the masses has been the sneers of a capitalistic mistress as exacting as she is icy.

The current state of affairs faced by these two women made them both well aware that, in the end, no matter what they did, the little guy would suffer. They were going to try and save people who lined up for their chains willingly and did nothing but meekly accept their fate. A demonstration here, a plea to an official there, an occasional hollow victory of sorts never really altered the equation that kept the majority enslaved and bound in servitude to the 1% who always came out on top in the end. That was the way of a world that had simply stopped trying to alter the equation. Mao had forced the upper class to work two years on farms and then come back to their jobs as executives, government officials and academics appreciative of how real people with real jobs had to work so hard to put food on their tables. It was a grand and glorious experiment in hope that unfortunately died with him and was buried forever.

J. Wayne Frye

PURSUIT

Still, Chablis and Lynton could not sit by and allow catastrophe to befall good people who, by chance of birth, had no hope. Chablis had figured out that the conspirators were hiding deep underground in an abandoned subway tunnel, but New York was full of them. The only hope was if Don called that night. So, promptly at 6:00PM she was by the phone number she had put in the classified section of the newspaper, anxiously awaiting a call that might help save a city and save the President from assassination.

In one of the few phone booths left in Manhattan, for the cell-phone conglomerates had signed their death knell with balmy greed, stood Chablis, waiting for the phone call that might signal a chance of avoiding catastrophe. The ring was a voice of hope, as she quickly picked up the receiver, Lynton jammed up next to her in the tiny booth, "Hello, hello!"

"It is I, Don, as promised, Chablis. What news have you?"

She carefully explained to him all that had occurred and then said, "Where is the hide-out for the conspirators? We must alert them that there are two C.I.A. moles among them and that their plan is playing into a vast conspiracy hatched by the C.I.A. to kill the President. They are using the anarchists to further their aims, and time is of the essence to avoid catastrophe."

PURSUIT

"Roy is the only one among us who knows," said an excited Don,

Chablis, very solemnly said, "Game time is 1:30 tomorrow. The tellurium is undetectable, so if they get to the stadium, all is lost, because the C.I.A. will do nothing to stop the assassination, only kill the perpetrators after the fact, but you know what? There is something else afoot, because why go to all this trouble to eliminate the President and then wind up with a Vice-President assuming office who is even more liberal."

"What is it Chablis?"

"Just a minute," said Chablis as she motioned for Lynton to go and buy a newspaper from the nearby stand by the building on their right.

Hurrying back with it in hand, there it was on the front page in big headlines – Vice-President to be at Waldorf Astoria Hotel in Manhattan to speak to Association of American Social Workers Convention. Speech at 1:30.

She said, "There is going to be a double assassination. The President and Vice-President are going down. Next in the line of succession then is the Speaker of the House, a Republican who has been beating the drums of war and promising more tax cuts for those at the top. This is big, really big. You guys have to get to me as soon as possible. No one will believe us, and anyway, with the C.I.A. in on the plot who do we trust?

Excitedly, Don said, "Manley, Roy and I will meet you at the IRT entrance on Lexington and 58th at 8:00 PM sharp. Come packing, they will resist, and make sure you aren't followed. As for the moles, all we can do is hope they have no way to communicate with their handlers."

Lynton stood in awe as Chablis dialled up Aaron and shared what was going to happen. Aaron told her to leave the V.P. to him. He was on it. Her job was to stop the main plot. He very stoically said, "Be careful girl, and make sure the dynamic dynamo is kept safe, too."

"Gottcha Aaron. You be careful, too."

There are the indignant of the earth, which give birth to hope in the midst of despair. Chablis had often had blood upon her brow, and though less so, Lynton had also known the sting of combat. Neither woman ever gave into fear. Lynton called Channa and Ingrid and said, "Ladies I am about to enter battle again, and I want you to both know I love you. I have tried to call Wayne, but cannot reach him. If I shall fall, let him know my last thoughts were of him.

Ingrid said, "We will be by your side in battle."

PURSUIT

"It is not necessary," said Lynton.

Ingrid replied, "Yes it is necessary. We have always stood together and shall any one of us fall, we all fall together. Where do we meet you and Chablis?"

These three had spilled the blood of evil ones.
They had suffered pain fighting Satan's sons.
To an accent unbowed, unrestrained these three
Stood mighty and unafraid with Chablis.

Women of the Philippines they are, heirs of glory.
Heroines of a bold and roaring Frye written story.
Nursed they from one mighty warrior mother,
Now they placed all faith and hope in one another.

Like mighty lionesses after a long slumber,
These three, with Chablis, are mighty in number.
Shaking all chains of restraint to earth like dew,
Look out miscreants, they are coming after you.

Night wrapped itself around the city as Chablis and Lynton waited for Channa and Ingrid, who showed up only a few minutes before the arrival of Don. Chablis met him at the IRT entrance by herself, as she wanted to avoid any chance of discovery. Don had the same precaution in mind as he showed up alone also. They both called their cohorts and all agreed to meet in the lobby of Hunter College at 695 Park Avenue. There, the seven met and adjourned to the cafeteria.

J. Wayne Frye   239

PURSUIT

Manley said, "What is freedom? We all have, since childhood, been suffering through slavery without realizing it, because the government has actually convinced most of us that slavery is freedom. I am appalled that we all fell into a trap that has been set by the C.I.A. to use us as dupes in their aim to inflame the populace and keep the people in bondage."

Chablis offered her opinion. "Work is required, but there is never enough pay except to keep us in food and shelter from day to day. We are all in a prison cell but don't realize it. Tyrants have the keys, and the servants of those tyrants are represented by the government. Right now, the C.I.A. is about to perform a coup d'état to wrest power from a Democratic President and Vice-President who have no will-power to stand up to our masters. Yet, the powers that be are still dissatisfied, because they want warmongering, right-wing, fascist, corporate loving Republicans in control so that they can further enslave the masses. We have a chance to prevent this coup d'état, but it will not be easy."

Roy blurted out. "I know where they are hiding and preparing for the destruction of Yankee Stadium and 50,000 people with one of the beacons retrieved from the Solomon Islands. But are you sure the C.I.A. is going to allow this to occur? It makes no sense for them to allow a conspirator to do this and escape with a beacon."

PURSUIT

Don concurred with Roy's assessment, but Chablis offered a more profound reasoning. "Believe me, the beacon will be used, and afterwards, the C.I.A. will have it, because the user will be the mole. Be assured, somehow they will find a Middle Eastern country upon which to pin the terrorist attack that cost the President his life, and, of course, the same will apply to the Vice-President's elimination. This is a plot more sinister than the lies about weapons of mass destruction in Iraq that the people willingly swallowed. That lie cost trillions of dollars and millions of lives. Believe me, this is going to be an even bigger deception."

"So, what do we do to prevent this? Are we to divide our resources between tackling those who are going after the President by the group we have disowned now and the C.I.A. who will be arranging the elimination of the Vice-President at the same time?"

Chablis replied. "No, my partner Aaron Adams, with his NYPD friend, John Havoc, no doubt, will thwart the attempt on the Vice-President, if at all possible. Our objective is to quell the anarchists and moles in the subway tunnel before they can set the plan in motion to destroy Yankee Stadium and the President along with it. First, we need to know where they are Roy."

Smiling, Roy coyly replied. "Near here."

J. Wayne Frye   241

PURSUIT

"How far," asked Chablis.

"Close enough to walk it. IRT at Lexington and 48th. Right near your place, Chablis."

"O.K., despite the fact I would like to see Yankee Stadium completely destroyed, as it is just another example of the city providing welfare to billionaires, we need to take these guys out where they are. If they get out, it is going to be more difficult to stop them."

Roy unfolded a paper napkin and began drawing the tunnel and the approach to it.

Stairs at entrance

Uptown line

←——————————

———————————
old storage shed → ▭

Chablis sighed and said to Roy, "How many of them there and do they have all three of the beacons?"

"Justin, Bruno, Lou, Bob for sure in the shed. All the beacons are with them."

Then Chablis released the bombshell. "Two of them are C.I.A. moles – Justin and Bob. Bruno and Lou are the primary targets then."

PURSUIT

Roy eased back in his chair and said, "Bastards."

"Welcome to real world, Roy. Nobody is what they seem, and when it all comes right down to it, money is the motivating factor that always destroys devotion to a cause," offered Chablis. She paused and then continued, "So, you think it is just four of them, nobody else there?"

Roy shook his head empathically. "I would say a sentry at the entrance and probably one near the storage shed but across the tracks on the train side. Too many and they call attention to themselves. Yep, six max the way I figure it."

Chablis took Roy's napkin and said, "The odds are good then, but how many of you are packing?"

Lynton, Ingrid and Channa shook their heads emphatically no. The three men at the table all nodded in the affirmative.

"O.K., four of our guns against their six, but the worst problem is that we go up against three of those damn beacons." Then she laid out Roy's napkin on the table and continued. "Lynton, I have seen how deadly you are with your heels. Your job will be to get the guy who is on the platform across from the storage shed. You neutralize him at my signal. Give him the kick of your life in the balls. Now, here is the big question. Can you kill him?"

J. Wayne Frye   243

Lynton thought long and hard. "Maybe, I'm not sure."

"No problem, I will be to your right. I'll pump him one to the head. We can't rely on maybes. It's OK, don't worry about it, but you have to get in close as I need that kick to disable him and make it easy for me."

"Done, Chablis."

"Ingrid and Channa. You two work your alluring magic. Distract the sentry and Manley, do you have a knife?"

"I do."

"O.K. Channa and Ingrid make sure the sentry has his back to Manley. Manley, place the knife to his back and then manoeuvre him quietly to a seat in the station. Slide the knife into him in the kidney area for instantaneous death that will be quiet. Leave him on the bench. Ingrid and Channa, you two move back to the outside of the entrance and watch for cops or any suspicious persons. Any thing looks suspicious start screaming 'murder, murder' and point to the dead guy on the seat. That will be our clue to haul ass. Now, Roy and Don you will move with me across the tracks once Lynton neutralizes the sentry across from the shed. Once you have killed the other sentry Manley, you join us."

PURSUIT

Chablis pointed out on the napkin where everyone would be.

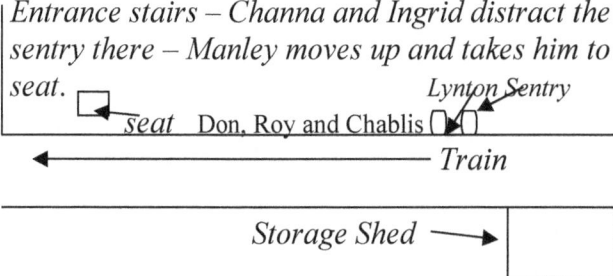

They all studied the map intensely and Chablis said, "Now, hopefully there will be very few people there. We wait until the train stops, people get off and get on obviously, which means there should be no more than a half dozen people around when we do this. The loud sound of the train leaving the station will muffle my shot to the sentry's head. Don, Roy and Manley, you three follow me rapidly across the tracks. My guess is they will have the shed bolted and probably padlocked. Roy, is the door thick? Can it be kicked in?"

"Very thin hollow-core door. We three men can easily kick it in."

"Great, you three kick it in, and I have my .38 in hand ready to do some damage. The beacons are what bother me. I don't even care about the piece of tellurium. If they aim the beacons, we are finished. My guess is they will not have them in their hands, so each one of you will spot a beacon and grab it. I will shoot anything that moves."

Roy said, "What do we do with the beacons once we have them?"

"Those things are not to ever get in anybody's hands, especially the CIA. The tellurium and the beacons are to be tossed into the East River. I will do it if I am alive. If not, or if something else happens, whoever is able must toss the beacons and the tellurium in the East River. You guys ready? It's almost ten o'clock. Let's rock and roll."

On their way out, Ingrid looked at Channa and said, "Damn, you know hanging out with Lynton can be dangerous."

Channa laughed and said, "Yeah, and we love every minute of it."

While all this was going on, Aaron and John were planning on how to avert the assassination attempt on the Vice-President. They could not involve any government agencies because they did not know who to trust. In fact, John was unwilling to bring in the NYPD; because of fear the C.I.A. had infiltrated their ranks.

Going directly to the Vice-President would be next to impossible, and contacting his aids was out, as there was no guarantee they were not on the C.I.A. payroll. In a nation that was under siege from its own government few alternatives existed.

Ironically, as Aaron and John walked down Park Avenue toward the Waldorf Astoria, they strolled by 695 Park Avenue, which was the location where Chablis and her crew of warriors had made their plans to assault the lair of the conspirators.

Aaron Adams was a man who personified what most men thought a man should be. Bold, brash, unafraid and unwilling to let the little guy be trampled on by the high and mighty in his presence, and above all, he was a man of action who never hesitated stepping forward with boldness to defend the downtrodden. Of course, his most endearing quality was his kindness that might not be as apparent on the surface, but beneath, in his heart, beat the rhythm of compassion that was always there to lend a helping hand to the those who had reached rock bottom in a world that was incessantly cruel. He was adored by many, but immensely feared by those of privilege, because he saw no man as privileged by virtue of position or birth. In fact, he found it appalling that in this day and age there were still kings, queens, princes, princesses, dukes and duchesses and even someone called Mr. President. How could any nation call itself a democracy and still have titled nobility in its ranks? And the worst offender of all was the

PURSUIT

U.S.A. where sports figures and movie stars were considered royalty, and then there was the leader of the country who was called Mr. President, which was an abomination in a nation that took so much pride in ballyhooing its grand democracy. Mr. President was no different than saying "Your Majesty," but this was the real America; the America no one wanted to admit was built on lies, deceit and hypocrisy.

With John Havoc, another bold defender of the downtrodden by his side, those who operated in quiet despair, or bowed before people to serve in menial positions, or were the children of mothers who had to endure winter winds of meekness in a land of plenty, found their nourishment of hope in Aaron Adams. While the rich and powerful tossed their dogs better food than that which the poor survived on, Aaron Adams was fighting the battle for justice in an unjust world. Now, he was ready to defend a man, whom he thought buffoonish, though the Vice-President did have a soft spot for the poor man, and had himself, rose from the ranks of the poor, and had never become wealthy off his public service. In fact, he was a rarity among the political class. He was but one man crying in the wilderness though, trying to alert the people to the ills of a society that based everything on economic riches rather than riches of the heart. Yes, this was a man who needed to be saved from those who saw him and the President he served as an impediment to the solidification of control by the privileged class. In fact, this was a person more devoted to the cause of the common man than the President, who also had come from humble circumstances. For an instant, Aaron thought that maybe he was actually saving the right one, and that Chablis should forget about her quest.

The USA was once a nation where the common man could walk up to the White House and ask to see the President, but now the President was part of the exalted, privileged class and that could no longer happen. The same applied for the Vice – President. You did not just run through the gauntlet of guards and say, "Hey, Mr. Vice-President, how about a word with you in regards to some people who want to blow your ass up?"

Aaron and John stood across from the Waldorf, just staring at the stately building as if waiting for a revelation from above to show them the way. Aaron turned to John and said, "The plot is in motion, but all we know is that somewhere the C.I.A. has someone ready to commit one evil act that will fell the man who, once the President is eliminated, stands between them and the Speaker of the House taking over the presidency and thus driving the final nail in the coffin of the common man, destroying the last vestige of hope in a nation that, for so long, has had so little hope. If we allow this to happen, the death bell has rung for the little freedom that is left."

PURSUIT

John seemed to be in deep thought. Aaron could see the wheels turning, so he just stood there in silence, waiting for what he hoped would be a revelation from his friend.

He did not have to wait very long. John, enthusiastically said, "Got it buddy. They will take him out simultaneously with the terrorists' killing of the President. Even a few seconds delay and the V.P. will be spirited away to safety once word of what happened to the President is immediately relayed. The time frame must be exact. Somebody the V.P. knows is going to carry this out, but how? How does someone do this and not get caught in the process?"

Aaron's eyes, beaming with recognizable assurance, said, "Easy, it will be one of the dignitaries at the gathering, someone who will be close by and simply press a button that will activate some type killing device. The Secret Service agent in charge of sweeping the room before the speech is, no doubt, a C.I.A. mole working with a dignitary who will be the trigger man or woman.

John said, "I got it. The dignitary activates the device upon signal that the President is dead."

Aaron was beginning to put all the pieces of the puzzle together now. "This is an intricate and complicated plot involving many higher ups in the government. My guess is that the Speaker of the House and several other prominent Republicans are involved in this damnable plot. We foil this plot and a huge house of cards is going to tumble, bringing to light an elaborate attempt at a coup d'état' by some very important people. This is bigger than anyone could imagine."

Then, Aaron stopped abruptly, thought for a second and said, "There is something we are all missing here, something to do with that damn hunk of metal and those three beacons. I just know it."

"'Tis to let the ghost of mental gold
Take from toil a thousand fold,
More than ever its substance could.
Ah, the evil ones trampled good.

Truth from government was a forgery.
Of the title deeds, which the people held,
There simply was no intrinsic worth,
As it was not the meek would inherit the earth.

The country's leaders had no soul.
All they wanted was control.
Over those who could not see
Tyranny was handed life's key.

And at length when you complain,
With a murmur weak and vain,
'Tis to see the tyrant's crew

J. Wayne Frye   251

PURSUIT

Ride with disdain over you.

Aaron felt an urge for revenge,
Blood of tyrants his brow to singe.
Blood for blood-and wrong for wrong:
Do thus those who are strong!

Aaron reached inside his coat and fondled his big bastard of a 45, caressing it like it was a lover. It was a death dealer that had many times brought destruction to those who dared challenge the man with no fear who could spit out justice in warm lead from the machine that made all men equal. He had long ago given up on a nation with no heart and no soul, but he had not given up on humanity, and as he watched the privileged and powerful plan yet another power play to maintain the control by the privileged class he asked himself what he could do to somehow exact retribution. Glancing over at John, who gave him a quizzical look, he said. "Fuck it. I'm taking all these assholes down. Go back to your job John, and go to your suburban home and enjoy life. I am about to fucking wreck havoc on the assholes who think they can practice tyranny with impunity. Not this time. This time they are fucking with Aaron Adams."

John knew that when Aaron was like this all hell was about to break loose. Not about to play it safe, he said, "Fuck my job, fuck my suburban home, fuck complacency. Let's do this buddy."

PURSUIT

Birds find rest in narrow nest,
When-weary of the winged quest;
Beasts find fare in woody lair,
When storm and ill are in the air.

Like swine, government officials litter spread,
And with fitting food are lavishly fed;
Each have a home and it is a fine one:
But the rabble in ghettos have none!

This is slavery-savage men,
Wild beasts within a forest den,
Would endure not as you do:
But such ills is all you knew.

"What art thou, Freedom? Oh! Could slaves
Answer from their living graves.
This demand, tyrants would flee
Like a dream's dim imagery.

Thou art not, as impostors say,
A shadow soon to pass away,
A superstition, and a name
Echoing from the eaves of fame.

Thou art clothes, and fire, and food
For the trampled multitude:
This country is not free
When so much poverty you see.

To the rich, Aaron, thou art a check;
When your mighty foot is on the neck

J. Wayne Frye

PURSUIT

Of the exploiters who will now quake
As you snap at them like a rattle snake.

Thou art justice – and never for gold
Will your righteousness be sold.
You are wisdom and freedom forever.
Ah, cock that 45 and pull the lever.

"You know what, Aaron," said a determined John, "ever since that supposedly humble man of the people was elected President I have waited patiently for him to make a move against the privileged class, but he has let them just keep laughing all the way to the bank. I don't know why any of us gives a damn about him being wasted. Yet, there is something in me that simply says no way, absolutely no way is there going to be another coup d'état like there was with Kennedy. I know damn well the C.I.A. took him out. Goddamn it, no way I am sitting idly by and watching it happen again. He may not be much, but he is a damn sight better than what lurks in the wings waiting to take over. The Speaker of the House is almost as big a buffoon as that idiot Bush who waltzed off with a huge pension for tanking the economy and lying us into war. What is the plan?"

"We are going to sweat Agent 88. We'll pull a little water-boarding exercise if necessary without pulling a rendition to some Third World cesspool. We'll see if he thinks water-boarding is torture.

PURSUIT

My guess is that, just like that asshole Cheney, when the chips are down, he'll fold up like an accordion. These chicken hawks always fold."

Aaron was wrinkled with age, but his intellect had not wrinkled at all, and his determination to never cower in fear before those who were exalted and arrogant never wavered. He was a man who was unafraid and un-bowing. As he and John stood across the street from the Melton Company headquarters he was actually hoping that Agent 88 resisted, because he loved bringing down the high and mighty. There was something extremely gratifying about watching those who felt superior grovel in fear.

Meanwhile, Chablis was preparing her warriors for battle as they carefully approached the Lexington and 48th subway entrance. As she had when she and Lynton walked toward the Melton Building with Aaron, she was feeling a certain exhilaration while looking at the high priced real estate that surrounded the street where they gallantly strode.

Those prison-halls of wealth and fashion,
Where no living soul feels compassion
For those who groan, and toil, and wait,
As must make their brethren pale.

You who suffer woes untold,
Or to feel, or to behold

J. Wayne Frye

PURSUIT

Your lost country bought and sold
With a price of blood and gold.

Let a vast assembly be,
And with great solemnity
Declare with measured words, that you
Are, no longer slaves, but free!

Be your strong and simple words
Keen to wound as sharpened swords,
And wily as serpents let you be,
For all the world to wearily see.

Chablis and Lynton stand tall
For you two shall give your all.
The rich and powerful see you now,
And before them you shall not bow.

Look out those who hide from the light,
Because these two have great might.
They fear not your monetary power,
For these two before that demon never cower.

The world would not understand the bright light
in their eyes, but they were certainly freer at that
moment in time than they had ever been, so free
that they were not hemmed in by the conventional.
Though all of them sympathized with the
anarchists, they could not sympathize with the
needless wholesale slaughter of innocents that was
about to occur, and within the enclave below

J. Wayne Frye   256

ground were two C.I.A. moles who were preparing to hand the country over to people much worse than anarchists. Once the Speaker of the House of Representatives was securely in the position of the presidency, the complete takeover of the country by the privileged class would be completed, and all pretence of fairness would be gone. This was a fight for the soul of the nation now.

PURSUIT

CHAPTER 12
DEVIL'S CALLING CARD IN MAC'S HAND

Let the tyrants pour sorely around
With a quick and startling sound,
Like the loosening of a raging sea,
Troops armed with money as a fee.

Let the charged artillery drive,
Till the dead air seems alive
With the clash of clanging wheels,
And the tramp of soldiers' heels.

Let their money be a bayonet
Gleamed with sharp desire to wet
Its bright point with commoners' blood,
But they shall not stop sanctity's flood.

Let the people arise from slumber,
And with a flash put the rich asunder.
Their money cannot save them,
For the rabble shall tear them limb to limb.

Stand revolutionaries calm and resolute,
Like a soaring forest close and mute,
With folded arms, and looks which are
Weapons of an unvanquished war.

And let panic, that out speeds
The speed of fast steeds,
Pass, a disregarded shade,

J. Wayne Frye   258

PURSUIT

Through a money phalanx dismayed.

Let the laws of the mighty land,
That were used for ill no longer stand.
Hand to hand, and foot to foot,
Destroy the rich in grand dispute.

The old laws of the nation - they
Whose revered heads with age are grey,
See now a grand and wiser day;
And liberty in every heart may lay.

On those who first should violate
Such sacred heralds in their state,
Rest the blood that must ensue,
And it will not rest on you.

And if then the tyrants dare,
Let them ride among you there;
Slash, and stab, and maim, and hew;
Be not ashamed of that you do.

With folded arms and steady eyes,
And little fear and less surprise,
Look upon them as they stay,
Till their evil has died away:

Then they will bow in shame,
To the place from which they came,
And the blood thus shed will speak
In hot blushes on their cheek.

J. Wayne Frye

PURSUIT

Every person in the land
Will point at them as they stand
They will hardly dare to greet
Their acquaintance in the street.

And the bold, true, brave warriors,
Who have hugged danger in rich foyers,
Will turn to those who would be free,
As a new day dawns for all to see.

And that slaughter to the nation
Shall steam up like inspiration,
Eloquent, oracular like a reigning Czar,
A volcano of liberty heard afar.

And these words shall then become
Like the oppressors thundered to doom,
Ringing through each heart and brain,
Heard again – again – again – again!

The oppressed rose like lions after slumber
In unvanquishable, undefeatable number.
Shake your chains to earth, like dew
Freedom is now meant for you.

What does it take to arouse the slumbering people? They sleep under the darkened sky with no hope, so they have already died. Those who suffer and moan in misery as a result of an evil system need to one day like sleeping corpses arise and throw off their pain to demand fairness.

J. Wayne Frye 260

PURSUIT

Standing across the street from the entrance to the subway station, Chablis and her mighty warriors prepared for battle. There was trepidation, but no one shivered in fear, as there was a feeling of exhilaration in the face of death. They knew what they were doing had great consequences for the future of the nation. Yet, they also knew that if they thwarted the coup d'état attempt, in the end the rich would still be on top and those at the bottom would still be trampled on by an unjust economic system. As always, the choice was between the lesser of two evils, and all you could hope for was that the total capitulation to the moneyed class with the Speaker of the House in power could be avoided. The moneyed class had won the economic war long ago, and all that could be hoped for was some temperance from those at the top. Maybe saving the President might actually make him finally take a stand against economic injustice and insist on some fairness. Many heads would hopefully roll and, no doubt, many in the moneyed class would be implicated in the coup d'état. Still, money and power would keep them from paying too high a price.

All the preparations had been gone over. Now was the time to execute with exact precision. Ingrid and Channa strolled across the street toward the guy at the entrance with their usual distinct penchant for the sensual that was like second nature to them.

J. Wayne Frye   261

PURSUIT

Chablis, Lynton and Roy were walking in front of Channa and Ingrid and seemed to attract little attention from the guy at the entrance as they ascended the stairs with Don and Manley close behind Channa and Ingrid. Ingrid stood at the entrance, and realizing that most men were always captivated by two women seemingly in lust, she leaned over and gently kissed Channa on the cheek affectionately. The guy lost his composure and in a flash, Manley moved up beside him with the knife and whispered, "Come with me."

He made no effort to combat Manley, but as they walked down the next to last step, he started to bolt. Manley adeptly shoved the knife into his kidney and he collapsed into Manley arms. He dragged him to the seat easily and sat him down. He sat beside him and waited for Roy, Don, Lynton and Chablis to make their move. Fortunately, there was only one person in the station, and as the train pulled in, no one got off, only the one guy got on, leaving the place empty of bystanders. The sentry at the far end immediately assumed something was amiss, so he started to pull his gun, but Lynton's heels of death were faster than he was. She buried her right heel in his groin and he tumbled over in excruciating pain just as the train pulled out of the station and Chablis pulled her 38 from her right garter where she kept it under her dress. One smooth motion and her hand was pulling the trigger before the sentry hit pavement. His brains splattered all over the far wall as Chablis motioned for Lynton to maintain her place while she, Roy, Manley and Don jumped onto the tracks and climbed up the far side to attack the storage shed. Before they could get to the building, two figures jumped out the door. Bob Swift and Justin Hartman had the beacons in hand. They dropped to their knees and aimed them at the attackers. Before they could get good aim, Chablis sent a special delivery made of lead that parted their scalps right down the middle. They tumbled over dead. Behind them, Bruno and Lou came out spitting lead. Again, Chablis, maintaining her cool, took careful aim and hit them both in the chest. However, they were obviously wearing bullet proof vests, as they only momentarily were stymied by the impact. Manley, with his knife out, hurled it through the air right for Bruno's face and struck him on the left cheek. With blood gushing out, Bruno moved to his left behind a barrel. Lou crouched down flat on the pavement as Chablis, Roy, Manley and Don were now stuck on the tracks, unable to move forward or retreat for fear of exposing themselves and becoming easy targets. At this point, everything seemed to become animated as Lou and Bruno had two quick-firing guns that vomited flame simultaneously and the echoing sounds of the reports in the tunnel were deafening. Another and another followed, until the air seemed to beat in waves around Chablis and the three men who were trapped on a track where a barrelling train would soon crush them beneath steel wheels.

PURSUIT

Then followed a rattle as the sound of the approaching train could be heard far down the tunnel. There was a small area near the shack which could serve as a buffer preventing them from being crushed, but to get there they had to cross an open area with the tunnel lights shinning down from above to their right and behind them, making them vulnerable to gunfire from Bruno and Lou.

Chablis looked back at the entrance and took careful aim, knocking out the nearest light with one shot. The other light was slightly around the corner and impossible to get a bead on.

Lynton knew what Chablis needed done, so she crawled along the floor toward the light. She got around the corner, knew she was out of sight of Bruno and Lou, so she sat-up against the wall and took off her shoes. She tossed the right one at the light and missed, and knew that since the light was in the line of fire, the next one had to do it or Chablis and the men would not be able to scurry to safety when the train pulled into the station. She took careful aim, and recalling how effective she was as a setter in volleyball, summoned all her skill to make a perfect toss that shattered the bulb. Instantly, Chablis and the three men ran under the overhanging lip and hid under the overhang as the train pulled into the station. Meantime, Bruno and Lou got the two beacons and moved quickly down the corridor with them in hand.

PURSUIT

A banging noise was heard and then footsteps vibrated above. There was a third party with Bruno and Lou, and he had apparently kicked a hole in the side of the building to escape. The train pulled out of the station as the three anarchists headed down the dark tunnel hugging the wall on the right tightly as they made their way over the one foot lip that made walking very treacherous. Suddenly, they dropped down on the tracks and Chablis and the three men were in hot pursuit. Seeing the back of one of the men, presumably the one who had just kicked a hole in the wall, Chablis motioned for her cohorts to stop so she could have complete silence and take careful aim. The bullet hit dead centre in the back, but the guy never even slowed down. Her puny 38 was no match for a bullet proof vest. Now, the chase was on, as the three anarchists rounded the corner and disappeared from view.

Horror of horrors, as Chablis and her crew walked up a flight of stairs and into the street they came up in Times Square and the throng that surrounded them shielded the anarchists. Chablis looked up at the giant digital clock in the square and saw it was 10 past midnight. She called Lynton and told her to take Channa and Ingrid with her and meet them at Starbucks on Times Square. The more help they had the better chance they might find the anarchists, but now they were lose in the streets, but the worst part of it was they were lose with the beacons and the tellurium.

J. Wayne Frye   265

PURSUIT

While all this was happening, Aaron and John were ensconced across the street from the Melton Building, waiting for a chance to apprehend Agent 88. He was the key to getting access to the V.P. Suddenly; the vibrating of Aaron's cell-phone alerted him to a call. Chablis let him know that things had gone array with the pursuit of the anarchists and that they were somewhere in Times Square loose with the beacons and the tellurium. Aaron left John to handle things on his own and made a hasty sojourn to Times Square to assist Chablis.

They all sat in Starbucks scanning the throngs of people moving by in hopes they might get lucky and spot the miscreants. Lynton, Channa, Ingrid and Aaron had to be provided with an idea of the way the three appeared, but as for the one who had kicked his way through the wall of the shed, Chablis was not sure, but she said that there was something familiar about his stride and the back of his head. She thought for awhile, but could not come up with an effective description other than the fact he was maybe 6:2, about 200 pounds (90 kilos) and had very broad shoulders and the strides of an athletic person.

Deciding to move onto the streets and look for the anarchists, they all fanned out through Times Square. Since Channa, Lynton and Ingrid were not armed, they paired off with someone who was packing. Thus began an all-night search.

PURSUIT

They met back at Starbucks every hour, but as the clock ticked toward 6:00 AM, they decided all was apparently lost as the sun began to rise. Then, Manley spotted something strange at the Times Square Hotel right across the street. He noticed a window on the 7th floor that kept having the shades opened and closed, as if there was a signal being relayed to someone. Sure enough, as they all watched, the blinds were flicking in a rhythmic fashion. Aaron and Chablis went across the street in front of the hotel and scanned the opposite side of the square for any indication that someone might be signalling back. At the Algonquin Inn on the far side of the square, another set of blinds on the 5th floor seemed to be blinking in a pattern. Aaron said, "We got 'um. You, me and the three guys nail 'um now. Lynton, Channa and Ingrid need to sit this one out."

"Gottcha, what is the plan of attack." replied Chablis.

Just then, Aaron noticed another strange thing occurring to their left. A large crowd was gathering around someone near the adjacent hotel. While still keeping his eyes on the windows where the conspirators were, he pulled Chablis along with him toward the commotion. It immediately became apparent there was a dignitary or celebrity who was causing the furor. Aaron leaned over and asked a lady who the person was. She looked back and said, "It's the Speaker of the House."

J. Wayne Frye   267

PURSUIT

Aaron and Chablis looked at one another and shook their heads. Everything was falling into place. The President and the Vice-President and now the Speaker were all in town, and the ascension to power would be a breeze as with the President and the Vice-President dead, the speaker would immediately take the oath of office and probably announce a tax cut for the wealthy along with an invasion of some Third World country while he was being sworn in. With the Speaker were three generals, so the plot probably went up the chain of command in the military, too. This was a plot so big that it might be beyond Aaron and Chablis' ability to foil. Yet, Aaron was determined to do all he could. He called John and gave him the news, telling him to sit tight unless 88 showed up, and then to give him a call. Meantime, he told Chablis, "You go to the Times Square Hotel and nail that son-of-a-bitch and get the beacon. Take Roy and Don with you. I'll take Manley with me and go to the Algonquin. The third one is still on the loose, but maybe we can get some information from these two if we don't have to kill them right away. Be careful."

It was easy to find the rooms as all you had to do was count the windows by the floor and you got the room location. Chablis, Roy and Don stood in the hallway of the Times Square Hotel, while across the street, Aaron and Manley stood by the door where Lou Swartz was waiting to hook up with Bruno at daybreak.

PURSUIT

They had to avoid killing the two, as they needed to locate the third man who undoubtedly had the tellurium and the third beacon. Chablis did not want to knock on the door for fear the reaction would be a hail of bullets from inside the room. She called Lynton and told her to send Channa to join Aaron and Ingrid to see her. She coordinated with Aaron and the plan was set. The two would try and lure the men out of their rooms with a ploy.

At exactly the same time, Ingrid and Channa eased next to the doors to the rooms and started shouting, "I'm not a cheap peace of pussy, asshole. You want me; you got to produce the goods. I haven't showed me anything yet."

Chablis moved to the left where the door would swing open, exposing Bruno, and Aaron did the same thing across the street. Sure enough, the doors eased open and the men had guns extended. The men, not seeing who was on their right, afforded Aaron and Chablis the chance to karate chop the extended arms. Before either man could fire the guns fell to the floor and the interlopers were inside and had them face down with knees in their backs so hard neither man could move.

Chablis shouted, "Move asshole and you're dead," as she cocked the hammer on her 38, which was against the back of his head. He lay there staring at the beacon that was on the bed.

PURSUIT

"O.K., ease up real slow," said Chablis, but he quickly rammed his head back against the gun, rolled over and tried to make it to the bed and the beacon. He simply didn't make it. One pop from her gun, which she purposefully aimed to wound, not kill, and he hit the floor about three feet short of the bed.

The bullet struck him in the left shoulder, and as he lay there bleeding profusely and breathing heavily, he said, "Ain't getting nothing outta me bitch."

Chablis eased up to him, again placing the gun at his head and said, "Getting nothing out of you, but I'm putting something else in you, another bullet asshole, and this time it is deadly. You want to live answer two questions, and we'll call the ambulance. Maybe they can stop the bleeding before your die from loss of blood. Frankly, I don't give a damn. Question one, who is the third guy who was in the shed?

"Fuck you bitch."

"Been done many times Bruno by lot better than you, but we'll skip that and go to number two. Where is he?"

"Who he is doesn't matter and as for where he is, I don't know. Go ahead, pull the trigger bitch. I ain't afraid to die."

PURSUIT

Pulling his head toward her, Chablis said, with a big grin, "No, but you might be afraid of torture." Then she looked over at Don and said, "Get the Dick Cheney special ready for him."

You could see the look of terror creep across his face. Whether it was the name Dick Cheney, which was synonymous with torture or the thought of the agonizing ordeal of water-boarding, he began to shake. The words were garbled but comprehensible. "I, I know where he is or where he will be."

"But who we talking about first," said Chablis.

"Hey, you fucked him. You should know."

Chablis, very nonchalantly replied, "Hey, I fuck everybody. May even fuck you if you survive. Who is he?"

He began to mutter, he got out M—a—c M—c –A—l—s—t—e—r. "

"Damn, I knew he looked familiar from the back. Mac McAllister."

Suddenly, Bruno went into cardiac arrest. Chablis did CPR, but it did no good. He just simply died. She got on the phone, told Aaron what happened and he said, "Ours is dead too. Sending the beacon over. Deep six both of them."

PURSUIT

He was thrilled to know she had gotten the name of the third conspirator, which he had been unable to do. He said, "Ball for this one is in your court. I am going back to help John with the V.P. Good luck Chablis. Stop that bastard! He is in possession of a weapon that is all-powerful."

"Will do."

Chablis knew she could trust Channa and Ingrid, so she told them to take the beacons and throw them in the nearby East River. Next up was to find Mac McAllister, the third beacon and the tellurium. It was 6:30 AM, and as the sun brightened to usher in the day, Chablis wondered if the day would end in darkness, the darkness of assassinations in a coup d'état' that was going to put a despot in the White House.

There is one political party in America that has always stood unabashedly against progress for the working man, always sided with the bankers and tycoons of industry, always supported the use of force against foes everywhere in the world, always supported corporate welfare but been against welfare for those wallowing in poverty, always believed that health care was a privilege not a right, always supported education only for those who could afford it, always believed that government should stay out of people's lives except when it comes to abortion and prayer, always believed that the right to firearms was more important than the right of victims to be protected from maniacal gun-toting 2nd Amendment-loving anarchists of hate, always believed that the poor were responsible for being poor and that low wages were necessary for businesses to compete, always thought blind faith should trump science, always believed they were the only party that truly loved America. The Republican Party was anathema to anything that helped the working man. Still the very people it trampled under iron-fisted ideology voted against their self-interest because they had been brainwashed into believing it was the party of the beloved Jesus, the party that stood for American arrogant exceptionalism and was a bulwark against the dreaded socialism that was the bane of free-enterprise which made American great.

Were the Democrats much better? No, not much, as the political system, thanks to a Republican appointee dominated Supreme Court had long ago made it possible for the rich to buy elections through decisions that let those with money give freely to politicians without restraint. So America had the very best government money could buy. It was a nation that offered government of the wealthy for the wealthy by the wealthy and everyone else be damned. For almost seven years now a Democrat had been President while the Legislative Branch was controlled by Republicans who had smarted all that time because they had lost the election, so they tried their best to make it almost impossible for government to function, putting up roadblocks to any legislation that might benefit the working men and women of the country. Still, they could not take the risk of waiting a little over a year for the next election, because one more day without complete capitulation to the privileged class was more than the nation could bear according to their convoluted thinking. There were just too many things the President could do during the brief time he had left in office that might actually tip the scales a bit too far toward social justice. The C.I.A., the military and Speaker could not allow a man who might actually get a backbone since he was at the end of his term of office to continue if there was anything that could be done to protect the status quo. For that reason, a coup d'état through assassination was what they saw as the only alternative. And as Aaron showed up outside the Melton Building, Agent 88, Brent L. Easton, came out of the building and he and John tailed him to the hotel where the Speaker was staying.

The Speaker of the House, a man who came from an upper middle class family and believed people had to be kept under control to serve the interests of business and religion was huddling with his three generals contemplating how once their selected assassin, Mac McAllister, had eliminated the President and how the C.I.A. would pop the V.P., they would be able to quickly consolidate things to make for a smooth transition to power for the Speaker. They did not like what they heard from Easton, as he explained how two lone P.I's had gummed up the well-oiled machinery of the coup, and he had to give-up McAllister to kept the lid on, because these guys were too smart to fall for a cover story. It did not matter, because McAllister was too far undercover to be discovered, and within a few hours mass destruction would rain down on Yankee Stadium while at the same time, he, himself, would see that the V.P. was taken out of the equation and John Havoc and Aaron Adams had been followed there by his three men, who would take them out. The two girls, Channa and Ingrid, were on their way to the East River, thinking they were dumping the beacons, but once there, two agents would dump the girls in the river and make-off with the beacons. Chablis, Lynton, Roy, Manley and Don would be eliminated with an assassination crew assigned by the C.I.A. Agents had discovered the bodies of the anarchists, so that would just be tied into the whole conspiracy theory. Once McAllister had brought down Yankee Stadium in a horrendous terrorist act, he would be eliminated by the C.I.A. which would keep the populace in the dark as to what really happened.

As they sat in Starbucks, Chablis looked across the street as the bodies they had left behind were very discreetly removed with no fanfare. The agency was keeping things under wraps. There would be no headlines about the deaths.

PURSUIT

The four agents assigned by Easton (Agent 88) to take out Chablis and her crew were just waiting patiently across the street from Starbucks. Chablis said goodbye to Channa and Ingrid, sending them off to the river to dump the beacons, but Chablis was no fool. The C.I.A. agents underestimated just whom they were dealing with. You see, Chablis very quietly said to Channa and Ingrid before they left, "You two have the beacons, so you are a target. Don't worry; they won't make a move until you get to the river, because there is where they will also dispose of you. I am going to follow you."

She moved very artfully to the washroom where she crawled out the window while the others stayed seated in order to keep the four agents across the street occupied. As she squeezed through the tiny window she cursed her overeating the past few weeks as she noticed her hips were larger than normal as she could barely get through. She walked down the alley and a guy leaning against the building said, "Hey baby. You a hot mamma. I got a big 'un for you."

Chablis replied, "Don't suck uncut and unwashed. Take a hike." Truth was she did suck uncut, but never unwashed.

She hit the street, mingled in with the crowd and watched Ingrid and Channa leave Starbucks, moving gracefully down Broadway meandering

PURSUIT

toward the East River with two of the four agents following. Meantime, the two agents still across from Starbucks suddenly realized that Chablis had been gone too long, so they figured she had somehow gotten out of Starbucks undetected and was following the other agents. They immediately split the scene to backup the other agents.

Chablis moved up near the two agents who were tailing Channa and Ingrid. As she approached them, they swivelled around, guns in hand, but Chablis was gone – disappeared from sight.

Perplexed, the two agents turned back to see that Channa and Ingrid had also apparently ducked down an alley. Just as they started to run toward the alley to their right, a voice called out, "Freeze assholes or die."

Still looking around, they did not see any sign of Chablis. By this time, the other two agents had caught up to them and there stood four bewildered professionals trying to figure out where Chablis was. Obviously, she had them in her sights, so they were reluctant to move. Ingrid and Channa walked out of the alley, went to the right and started down the street as Chablis said, "No, no boys, follow them and you'll be picking up your guts off the sidewalk."

They stood there, still trying to figure where she was, but afraid to move. Down the street from them, they noticed a metal awning over a window. Chablis had somehow managed to elevate herself enough to grab the overhang and boosted herself up on the top of the awning. One of the agents said, "Fuck it" and went for his gun.

Chablis squeezed off one round and his head exploded like an over-ripe watermelon, scattering brains on the two guys to his right and the one to his left. The three guys left pulled their guns in a futile exercise, as Chablis squeezed off three quick rounds and they dropped like bowling pins hit with a five pound bowling ball.

Channa and Ingrid, scared as they had never been in their lives, glanced back and saw the men lying on the pavement as Chablis jumped down from the awning and waved them on. She shouted, "Drop those beacons in the East River and head back to your hotel. Your part in this is over."

Chablis headed back toward Starbucks and when she got there two agents were standing by the doorway. Chablis whispered as she went in, "Me 4, you guys 0. Want me to run up the score some more?"

They started to go for their guns, but Chablis had a secret weapon by her side. Lynton had gotten up, and walked to her right. The dynamic dynamo simply raised her right heel as she pivoted on her left leg and buried it so deep into one guy's stomach that she thought it was stuck. The other guy could not get his gun out before Chablis had artfully used the heel of her right hand to crush his nose and he tumbled to the pavement. Roy, Don and Manley were up and out the door in an instant. The five of them quickly moved across the street as mayhem ensued around Starbucks. Agents suddenly began to converge on them from all over. The jig was up it appeared, but Chablis motioned for them to follow her up Broadway. Within seconds there was a mass pursuit and a few shots rang out as the agents showed complete disregard for the safety of civilians who were scurrying for cover.

They made it to the MTA subway at Times Square and 42nd, quickly moving down the stairs and just catching the last car as it was pulling out of the station. As the door closed, the agents stood dumbfounded just staring. Chablis smiled and waved at them.

It was now 12:30 PM and it would take them 52 minutes to get to the Bronx where the train stopped right across from Yankee Stadium. They sat down and Chablis called Aaron to fill him in on what had gone down. Aaron had observed Agent 88 (Brent Easton) entering the hotel where the Vice-President would appear in a few minutes. It was beginning to look as if all had been lost. Chablis and her cohorts were stuck on a train that was only going to get to Yankee Stadium a few seconds before chaos would rain down on unsuspecting masses, including the President. It appeared that a coup-d'état was about to be successfully pulled off by the conspirators and the blame would land on anarchists rather than the C.I.A., the Speaker of the House, and at least three generals. The stage was set for all power to be ceded to a small group that would institute, without hesitation, a system that would no longer hide in the dark corners of power, but blatantly assert the supremacy of a small clique of billionaires, military leaders and, a religious hierarchy that would make the nation an economic and religious theocracy. This was what the Republicans had dreamed of for years.

Aaron and John had no way to reach the Vice-President, as the America of the day had become so schizoid that government officials had to be isolated from the people they were supposed to represent. Fear of radical Islamists and political nuts was so pronounced that anxiety reigned like a king on a throne of paranoia. The U.S.A. was a nation that, as a whole, needed to be on a psychiatrist's couch to have its psyche of fear psychoanalyzed.

Aaron and John had a plan that might just work if all things fell into place properly. The V.P. was to take the back entrance where he would be free of public scrutiny, so there was no way they could get to him before or during his speech. However, if they could create a big enough commotion outside the hall, perhaps they could interrupt the plans to kill the V.P. However, all their plans went down the toilet once they saw who was showing up for the speech. Instantly, as the man got out of the car, they knew who was assigned to take out the V.P. Lena Langley was clutching the arm of Pearson Adelson. She looked over at the two and smiled, but Adelson had a different reaction. He dropped his hold on Lena and looked toward John just as Agent 88 (Easton) walked up to greet the two. Adelson obviously was going to be the trigger man, because no one would suspect him, the Police Commissioner. He would just stroll out the door or even help with the investigation once the task was completed.

Chablis and her crew hopped off the train and walked up the stairwell to East 161st Street and River Avenue right in front of Yankee Stadium.

It was 1:23 PM and the sun was shining intensely. Chablis looked up at the glistening stadium and thought what a colossal, garish, ostentatious monument to greed and misplaced priorities. George Steinbrenner had blackmailed the city into building the monstrosity so his progeny could rule like potentates over an empire funded by a city that had rather hand money to a billionaire than to the poor who were living on the streets. This was America at its best. This was the America that always managed to hand lavish welfare to those who needed it least and deplore welfare for those on their knees begging for a hand up from a society that laughed at poverty and scoffed at those trapped in it as if somehow they were responsible for their predicament rather than the economic system that was always skewed to favour the rich.

There was a pall of intense uncertainty that seemed to hang over all of them as they stood in perplexed silence as they surveyed the scene. They had made it to the stadium, but what good was it going to do?

Roy was gazing around trying to spot anything out of the ordinary. Don said to him, "Damn," as he looked at his watch, which had just jumped to 1:28. "What are we looking for? What can we find that is out of the ordinary?"

Chablis surveyed the street up and down, eyeing the entire area with intensely keen astuteness while her dear friend, Lynton Viñas, who had never seen such a huge sports complex before, stood there staring in awe at what simply seemed like a giant concrete pit that was filled with screaming fans anxiously awaiting the privilege of watching a pack of arrogant, bombastic over compensated prima donnas parade around in uniforms acting like they were actually doing something that contributed to the improvement of mankind.

PURSUIT

Behind Lynton was the entrance to the stadium. She began to stroll, along with the rest of her friends, down the street to the right of the stadium. There was a slight indentation into the sidewalk about 100 feet up the street.

Indentation Area

The walk up the street was very slow and deliberate. Chablis, with a foreboding sense of anticipation, could not take her eyes off that slight indentation, and then she looked down the street and saw a lone yellow cab working its way through traffic, heading their way. It was moving from the far left lane into the right lane, heading toward the indented area. Chablis signalled for them all to halt right where they were.

The cab pulled into the indented area and a man got out. Chablis shouted "damn." It was Mac McAllister with the beacon in his hand. He took immediate aim at Manley and the beacon gave off a low hum and Manley disintegrated into dust. He pivoted the beacon toward Don and within an instant Don was gone.

Chablis and Lynton quickly ducked behind some trees to their right as Roy ran toward the stadium. He would never run again. The devil had come calling, and his calling card was in Mac's hand.

CHAPTER 13
WOULD THEY OR WOULDN'T THEY?

Mac McAllister looked at his watch and decided to ignore Chablis and Lynton as it was 1:30 – zero hour at the proverbial ground zero that would be talked about by the media, the politicians, the man-on-the-street as the time when America was once again attacked by those who deplored all that wonderful liberty it supposedly had. It would be another rallying cry to rouse the populace to line-up in unison to support wars and torture to bring those evil-doers to justice. 9/11 would only be a footnote to what was about to happen.

Chablis had gun in hand and was using a tree as cover; although, she asked herself what good was it against a weapon as powerful as that damn beacon. Lynton hugged the ground next to Chablis and said, "What do we do?"

Puzzled, Chablis replied, "Damned if I know," as she peeped around the corner looking for Mac. He was gone.

Suddenly, the great tower entrance to Yankee Stadium had fallen on the small crowd at the entrance, bruising into jelly a legion of buried wretches, and then beating into ruins the whole mass of the stadium which crumbled into a pile of dust, bent metal and broken concrete.

J. Wayne Frye   285

PURSUIT

Every outlet from the neighbourhood was being furiously fought for, hordes of screaming, shrieking madmen were crushing and stamping people into heaps, and with the growth of each writhing heap the ghastly confusion rapidly accelerated. Building after building was collapsing around them. Apartment buildings were falling and walls were being driven asunder as the shells burst within them.

But this spectacle, grievous of its kind, was as nothing compared to what Lynton's and Chablis' eyes, riveted in disbelief, observed occurring all up and down the nearby streets. Frantic women, with babies in their hands, were trodden down in what was a growing mass massacre of hysteria. Fires began to burst out on all sides as terrified throngs scurried about with no understanding of what was occurring. Pandemonium had reared its ugly head in the Bronx, and unless Chablis did something quick, the destruction would gradually spread across the entire city.

Huge circles of roaring flames raged violently all around Chablis and Lynton, who both remained perfectly calm while all about them people panicked, screamed and ran in disarray. The emphasis on the news would be the death of the President, but the real people, the ones who genuinely counted were dying in mass before the two women who felt helpless and useless as the carnage continued.

PURSUIT

Where was Mac while this feverish and scorching devastation spread like a wildfire of misery? The sky, now overcast with dark clouds of rising dust and black with soot up rolling like smoke wreaths signifying the loss of hope, had made sight difficult as Chablis blinked, blinked, blinked and blinked to try and get a focus on where the destructible beacon was that was causing all the devastation.

Suddenly, to her right, standing between two cars, she spotted Mac with a look of delirium manifested across his soot-covered face. On the trunk lid of the car to his right laid the piece of tellurium. His head was tilted slightly to the right, as if he was listening to instructions from that damnable hung of metal. In his right hand was the beacon which he was deftly scanning toward anything left standing.

Chablis concentrated intently on Mac as she took aim in his direction. A crash of the one column left standing from the stadium momentarily distracted her. The column vanished into a pile of dust, and a stream of fire like a comet's tail drew out instantaneously in the wake of the fallen column and it swiftly moved across the pavement in front of Chablis lighting the gas tanks of the cars parked nearby, causing huge flames to soar skyward. She had to end this carnage, so she refocused toward the two cars where Mac stood, but he had disappeared.

J. Wayne Frye 287

PURSUIT

Meantime, the flames from the exploded gas tanks spread like molten lead, its contents shooting over the shrieking throngs nearby. For a full fifty feet the blaze filled the roadway, and the mob, lapped in flame, was writhing and wrestling within it. Another resounding ear-rattling explosion violently hurled Chablis and Lynton onto the sidewalk to their left about twenty feet from one another as they were now sprawled in disbelief before the running hordes that trampled everything in their paths.

They remained, in shock, lying for some time where they were. But the end of the carnage was not at hand. The two of them rose and staggered toward one another, grasping each other in fright. They had to get away from the hysterical throng before they were trampled in the mass melee of mayhem.

The fires were blazing and a crimson yellow rim stretched all the way from them to what appeared to be at least 5 kilometres (about 3 miles) in every direction. There were visible blazing circles all about them as doom and hopelessness were apparent to all left alive.

At the exact same time that Chablis was tackling the Mac McAllister situation, Aaron and John were in front of the hall where the V.P. was to speak. They began to start fighting one another in order to create a disturbance.

PURSUIT

Pearson Adelson was the key, so as the doors to the hallway opened and two Secret Service agents stepped out, Aaron shouted, "bomb, bomb, Adelson has a bomb."

Without hesitation, the agents ignored Aaron and John and ran toward Adelson who was on the dais three chairs down from the Vice-President. He was too far away to reach, so they simply shouted "bomb," which made the V.P.'s bodyguards immediately shield him and they quickly ushered him out of the room to safety. Agent 88 was standing in the back of the room, and in order to make sure Adelson did not spill the beans, he quickly made his way toward the front of the room, pulled his gun and shot Adelson in the head as he pointed to his left pocket and said, "bomb trigger."

Lena Langley, who was beside Adelson, made a quick move to her right, rolling on the floor to avoid the mayhem. Aaron and John noticed Agent 88 move toward the side door and quickly exit. No doubt, he was going to alert the Speaker of the House and the generals that the plot had been foiled.

Aaron and John very quietly blended in with the fleeing crowd and headed toward Times Square, where they planned to dispense some personal justice to the conspirators who were, no doubt, trying to figure a way to explain all this.

J. Wayne Frye 289

PURSUIT

Lena, completely unaware of what her date for the day had been up to would have some explaining to do the Secret Service, but she would eventually be cleared of any suspicion or complacency in the plot.

As Aaron and John were frantically trying to get to Times Square, Aaron called Chablis to let her know that the President might be lost, but that the Vice-President was in a secure place, and it appeared the nation would be spared the presidency of a fascist. Chablis said, "Thanks. Can't talk now. I have to find Mac and the tellurium. Great work Aaron. Sorry I let you down."

"You let no one down Chablis. Get that son-of-a-bitch and deep-six the tellurium and that damn beacon."

Aaron and John were at the hotel, and fleeing like geese after a gunshot had been heard were the Speaker and the generals. They had even dispensed with security, as they were so frightened at what was coming down that they were piling into a limousine waiting by the curb. Agent 88 tapped on the window and spoke to the Speaker, and as he did, he placed a piece of magnetic metal on the side of the door. He nodded at the Speaker and apparently said something to the generals. The car pulled away. Aaron and John looked at one another, knowing what was coming.

PURSUIT

Agent 88 looked back at Aaron and John who were perhaps one hundred feet away. He smiled as he removed a small remote control device from his left coat pocket. He pressed a button on the device and a mighty explosion could be heard down 42nd Street. Aaron and John looked over their shoulders at the limousine which was nothing but a smouldering hunk of metal. 88 was trying to eliminate all lose ends. Then, he gave Aaron and John a huge smile and eliminated one more lose end. He placed his gun to his temple and pulled the trigger.

Chablis and Lynton were desperately trying to locate Mac as they methodically moved down the street among all the mayhem. Men and women were being crushed, trampled on, and suffocated under debris. While all this was happening, Chablis and Lynton had moved to the centre of the street and just kept moving forward. Chablis remembered that old saying, "never slow down, just keep moving forward."

Rushing up the street, their calmness was in direct contrast to the frenzied masses scurrying around them. As they moved forward, thinner grew the groups, and finally they came upon a horse that had obviously been abandoned by a mounted policeman who was either helping the throngs of frightened people or maybe had been killed in the melee. Hastily grabbing the harness, Chablis pulled herself up on the steed and reached down to give Lynton a boost up behind her. What a sight, two women riding on horseback among all the turmoil and destruction.

They kept moving up the street, when suddenly, a strange group off to the left caught their attention. Two men had just entered a small park, followed by a third. The first two men were talking excitedly, and pointed at intervals to the rising smoke down the street. Bob Ramson, the Republican politician and none other than Art Carson, the man who had taken Chablis to meet Nesmond Nimrod were the two men, but the third man made her gallop the horse behind two nearby cars parked on the street and dismount with Lynton. Chablis placed two fingers over her lips to indicate they needed complete quiet. The third man was the surprise. There he was, Mac McAllister, carrying a large bag, no doubt with the tellurium and the beacon in it.

Hiding between the two cars, Chablis and Lynton observed a very animated conversation. Obviously they had heard that the plans had gone array as the V.P. had escaped. The whole conspiracy was coming unravelled and many heads were going to roll. Mac obviously elected to protect himself by eliminating anyone who might be able to point the finger at him. He did not reach for the beacon, but rather pulled out a revolver and instantly killed the two men, who were obviously co-conspirators in the plot.

PURSUIT

This was a very delicate situation and Chablis wanted to make sure she did not miss this time. Letting him get away with the beacon and the tellurium was not an option. With that kind of power, the conspirators would be back for a second go in no time, and even if the government got its hands on those two items, they would be used to promote American greed all over the world, a world that had already fallen far too deep into the evil of corporate control.

Discretion, not foolish valour was necessary to assure that this threat was eliminated for all time. Mac knew that he was the man now with all the power as the other conspirators were dead or awaiting their fates. He arose and started to move back toward the area where he had wrought devastation. The mobs were still screaming, but Mac moved adroitly through them with Chablis and Lynton trailing inconspicuously behind.

The wretched victims were fighting to get to safety without realizing the destruction was over. Pandemonium was still rampant as heaps of butchered and trampled bodies tripped up the frantic survivors in batches as they ran. Among all the mayhem, Mac simply strolled as if he were out for an afternoon walk as Chablis and Lynton moved stealthily behind him. The cloudy pall above, the still smoking and ruined structures and the heaving crowd with its multitudinous detail of slaughter, suffocation, and writhing, the smoke-clad hulks of smouldering cars all dotted the landscape.

Yet, there seemed an angry majesty to all the destruction, almost as if it was just a sign of a nation that never seemed to be able to come to grips with its own evil. It could only see the evil of the outside world, because it was unwilling to look in the mirror that reflected where the true evil was.

There seemed to be a morbid air of pleasantness emanating from Mac. The massacre had been swift and short, but he appeared proud of what he had wrought on a nation that had dished out much more horror than it had ever suffered. Were the chickens now coming home to roost?

This was an opportunity of sorts for America. It could look within and try to come to grips with what it had brought upon itself, or it could once again point the finger of condemnation at others. The later was far more likely.

Onward past the ruins of Yankee Stadium the three walked as if the thousands of wounded and dying who littered the area all around them and whose cries were penetrating the humid afternoon air did not exist. These three were in a parallel universe summarily cleared of all the pain and suffering, void of any semblance of the misery that was all around them. They were walking though hell, but were spared the roaring fires that were consuming everything around them.

Suddenly, Mac stopped, and so did Chablis and Lynton. He placed the bag down beside him, dropped to one knee and brought out the beacon in his right hand. He dropped onto his right elbow and suddenly pivoted onto his back and sat up, beacon aimed at Chablis. He smiled as he shouted, "You're a hell of a woman Chablis."

He started to press the button on the beacon, but before he could, Chablis pulled the trigger and a large hole opened up right between Mac's eyes. He was still smiling as he slumped over and dropped the beacon.

Chablis picked up the beacon and Lynton grabbed the bag with the tellurium in it. They did not speak to one another. They simply walked and walked and walked until they got to Throggs Neck, where they tossed the beacon and the tellurium into the river.

Aaron and John spent several days detailing all they knew to the Secret Service. They, along with Chablis, Lynton, Ingrid and Channa were told that any mention of what they knew would be a breech of the Patriot Act, and even Filipinos were subject to the act. Keeping the lid on the attempted coup d'état was in the national interest as it was imperative the people not know how close they came to having their government overthrown.

PURSUIT

The Hudson sisters had gone to the New York Times as promised, but the paper refused to believe them and did not print their story.

Old Robert Hernandez had closed out Donald Perez's estate and disseminated the money to Lynton, Chablis and Lena. Losing his son for a second time was more than he could handle. Two days after giving the girls their checks, he went into his bedroom one evening and shot himself in the head.

At the airport, there were emotional goodbyes as Lynton, Ingrid and Channa bid farewell to Aaron, Lena and Chablis. As the plane took off for Manila, Aaron heard Lena say to Chablis, "Come on girl. Isn't it time you took a little trip to the wild side?"

Chablis took her hand and they strolled out of the airport together as Aaron stood there wondering. Would they or wouldn't they?

PURSUIT

EPILOGUE
ONLY TIME WILL TELL

On a desolate, lonely island in the Pacific, a lone figure made its way beneath the surface of the sea where the ship called the Bounty had rested for almost 250 years. There was an object in the captain's cabin that possessed infinite power. It was one of two pieces of tellurium removed from a dinghy that had been attached to a ghost ship. No one but the captain had known that he had removed two pieces of the precious metal from the dinghy, and that secret had been maintained until it was retrieved that day by a lone diver into the wreck, a member of the Pitcairn community who was just simply curious.

The man carefully removed the tellurium from the cabin and brought it to the surface. He put it in a reed basket and took it to his home.

Up until that day, the sinister object had laid quietly in the captain's cabin, and the 49 people who currently called the island home had lived a peaceful, quiet life free from the evils of the outside world except for that brief period of time when things fell apart after someone had brought a similar object home from a dark cave on the far side of the island.

The diver looked at the object that came from far, far away long, long ago that he had now

J. Wayne Frye

brought into the light of day, and things might or might not change on the island. Only time will tell.

THE END